SINGING WIRES

OTHER FIVE STAR WESTERN TITLES BY L. P. HOLMES:

River Range (2006)
Roaring Acres (2007)
Riders of the Coyote Moon (2009)

SINGING WIRES

A WESTERN STORY

L. P. HOLMES

FIVE STAR

A part of Gale, Cengage Learning

GALE
CENGAGE Learning

Detroit • New York • San Francisco • New Haven, Conn • Waterville, Maine • London

GALE
CENGAGE Learning™

LIBRARY OF CONGRESS CATALOGING-IN-PUBLICATION DATA

Holmes, L. P. (Llewellyn Perry), 1895–
    Singing wires : a western story / by L.P. Holmes. — 1st ed.
        p. cm.
    ISBN-13: 978-1-59414-944-3 (hardcover)
    ISBN-10: 1-59414-944-5 (hardcover)
    I. Title.
PS3515.O4448S56 2011
813'.52—dc22   2010051986

First Edition. First Printing: April 2011.
Published in 2011 in conjunction with Golden West Literary Agency.

Printed in the United States of America
1 2 3 4 5 6 7 15 14 13 12 11

ADDITIONAL COPYRIGHT INFORMATION

CHAPTER ONE

Riding the high box of a double-hitch Russell, Majors & Waddell freight wagon outfit, Clay Roswell came into Fort Churchill, Nevada Territory during the sunset hour of a hot July day. On the box at Roswell's right, teamster Bill Yerkes used copious profanity and a deft jerkline to guide dusty mules and wagons through a vast tangle of activity to a final halt beside a great spread of freight corrals. Then he pointed with his whip.

"You'll find the office of Alex Majors at the far end of that warehouse yonder, son. He's a busy man, but an easy one to talk to. I doubt you're going to have much luck, but it won't hurt to ask."

Roswell said—"Obliged for the lift, friend."—and climbed down, pausing as he reached the ground to stretch the stiffness of a long ride from his muscles.

He had a Texan's tallness, with the lean flanks and compact hips of a man grown up in the saddle. His chest had a good lift and his shoulders were square and solid. There was a touch of the aquiline in his features, giving them an alert, forceful cast. His skin had the burned darkness of a desert man and against it his eyes were stone gray and tempered with a certain taciturn reserve. Under the pushed-back brim of his battered old hat his hair lay, thick and tawny, pretty well hiding the line of a not-too-ancient scar above his right temple. In his veins the vigor of twenty-seven years burned strongly.

So this, he mused, was Fort Churchill, western gateway to

7

the desert stretch of the Pony Express. A wild frontier town, boiling with dust and action and the tumultuous fever of a nation on the move. Here, where he stood, was the eastern fringe of the town, while beyond the northern limits lay the military post. And up there, even as Roswell had his good look around, the flag was floating slowly down from its tall mast, while a bugle sang retreat in a high, sweet tenor.

Roswell circled the sprawling swing of the corrals, dodged lumbering wagons and sweating, laboring strings of mules. The tumult and action seemed endless. Whips snaked out, cracking. Teamsters yelled at their mules, yelled at each other, and swapped curses with indiscriminate profligacy. After the long, hot quiet of the desert, this place was pure bedlam in Roswell's ears.

Things seemed to open up a little more off to the right and Roswell moved out that way. Here towered long piles of slim, tapered poles, freshly cut and peeled, still oozing resin, the tang of which cut through the dust and touched the nostrils with a hot, piney fragrance. Several wagons were pulled up, either unloading or waiting to unload more of the poles, and it was as Roswell paused to watch for a moment that the girl came into sight.

She made a quick, light-stepping figure, sturdily clad in half boots, short skirt, and open-throated blouse. Her bared head gleamed like beaten copper in the sun's last radiance. She stopped beside a tallyman who was making some entries in a notebook. She stood talking to him, her feet slightly spread, her hands on her hips in a manner almost boyishly free and untrammeled.

Clay Roswell's appraisal of her was frankly one of interest and approval, for since leaving the Mormon settlements around Great Salt Lake several months before, he'd seen few women, and these were all older, wives of men who tended and worked at some of the lonely Pony Express way stations scattered across the desert, women grown gaunt and drab and silent from the solitary hardships they had endured. Against them, this girl's glowing youth was in strong contrast. She seemed to feel Roswell's glance, for she turned and met it for a long moment, while deepening color stole across her cheeks. Then she turned her back and went on conversing with the tallyman.

An unloaded wagon pulled away from a pole pile and a loaded one creaked up and took its place. A couple of men swarmed up, pry bars in hand, and began loosening the chains that held the load in place. The girl and the tallyman turned and started to move away. And it was at this moment, as the retaining chains clanked to the ground, that a poorly placed pole on the wagon began to slide.

For an inanimate thing, it acquired a sudden malevolence. It became a thing alive, vicious and beyond control. It came off the wagon with a bounding twist, struck the earth, and then lashed forward in a wicked, rolling charge. The girl and the tallyman, their backs turned to all this, had no slightest inkling of what was coming at them.

A frantically dodging wagon man yelled a strangled warning, but his shout was lost in the general uproar of activity around about, and neither the girl nor the tallyman paid it any attention. Clay Roswell didn't yell; he just acted. It was instinctive, without conscious thought, just as a man out of pure reflex might dodge an unexpected blow coming his way.

In two long leaps he was beside the girl. He caught her up bodily and tried to jump over the crazily charging log. He got almost clear. The log clipped one foot, twisting him off balance, spilling him and the girl. As Roswell fell, he heard a man's hard, startled, agonized cry.

Roswell took most of the impact of the fall on his right side and shoulder, but the girl, cushioned in his arms, knew no hurt at all, except to her startled dignity. Sizzling with bewildered anger and outrage, she tore loose from him, and, when she gained her knees, slapped him twice across the face as hard as she could hit.

"You . . . !" she raged. "You'd dare . . . !"

Before she could say more, one of the unloading crew was there to lift her to her feet, exclaiming anxiously: "Miss Kate! You're not hurt? That pole . . . it got away!"

Now came the tallyman's anguished cry again, this time in coherent words. "My leg! That pole . . . it broke my leg!"

The girl whirled, stared, ran over there, with several of the workers at the pole pile hurrying to join her. Clay Roswell got to his feet, one of them still numb from the pole's impact. His lean jaw burned, his head buzzed from the slaps he'd taken. Lord! What a wildcat!

The group thickened about the luckless tallyman, caring for him. There was nothing Roswell could do to add to their efforts, so, limping a little, he headed once more for the warehouse Bill Yerkes had pointed out for him. He'd gone but a little way when a breathless cry stopped him.

"Please . . . !"

It was the girl, hurrying up to him. Her face was pale, her eyes very big. She began to stammer a little.

"I . . . I didn't know . . . I didn't realize. I'm sorry I . . . I slapped you."

Dry humor quirked Roswell's lips. "I know. Forget it. We were both lucky."

Close up, Roswell thought, she wasn't exactly pretty. But she was—well—good-looking because all the brown vigor and health of a wide land's sunshine and free air was in her, and he had never seen eyes more clear and faultless. Color began to steal back into her cheeks.

"Of course I thank you greatly. That pole. . . ."

"Sure." Roswell nodded. "Treacherous brutes, once they get on the loose. I hope that fellow yonder is not hurt too bad. Sorry I couldn't have got him clear, too."

She gave him another long, straight look, then murmured— "Thank you again."—and went back to the group about the tallyman. Roswell went on his way, walking steadily now, the numbness leaving his foot.

At the door of the Pony Express office, Roswell paused, hesitating over moving into the obvious rush and hurry about the place. They'd have little time for him in there, probably. But as he thought back over the long months and all he'd gone through to get here, his jaw stole out in stubbornness. A man never knew about anything until he asked, and all they could do was tell him yes or no. So he squared his shoulders and went in.

Here indeed was busyness. Teamsters just in from the lonely way stations along the hazardous trail reporting on loads of supplies successfully delivered. Other teamsters, about to head out on that same long trail with loaded wagons, getting final instructions. Clerks and warehousemen, hands full of lists and waybills and other paperwork, hurrying in and out, arguing and haggling over some disputed item or place of delivery.

Then there were several express riders, either off duty or waiting to take over a relay. All young, these riders were, lithe and sun-blackened, saddle sure and full of youth's reckless courage and hardihood. They smoked and swapped idle conversation and their smiles were quick and in their eyes lay the prideful glint of men involved in spectacular and dangerous and vastly important business.

A great deal of the activity revolved around a raw-boned man with a rippling black beard, sitting behind a desk in one corner of the room. There was power and authority and crisp ability in this man. His voice was deep, his orders short, blunt, and to the point. He seemed to be able to take in the substance of a report or a supply list with a glance, and then he would initial these with one quick drive of a big hand. This, decided Roswell, was undoubtedly the man he wanted to see and speak to. He backed up against a wall, out of the way, and waited his chance.

From outside, just a growing echo cutting through the solid rumble of other activity, came a note that held a thread of excitement in it. A shaggy-headed hostler pushed part way in at the doorway.

"Pony Bob Haslam coming in," he reported. "Jay Kelly, your mount's ready."

A dark, wiry rider moved toward the door. "All right, Shad."

Aside from Roswell and the man at the desk, all others in the room followed the swarthy rider outside, a gleam of anticipation in their manner. And this, Roswell fully understood. He'd seen the same thing happen many times at relay stations across the desert stretch. The arrival and departure of the express, no matter how many times a man might witness it, never lost its lifting thrill. It was always a high point. For even the most unimaginative of individuals understood that this thing was epic, and they wanted to be spectator to it, or some small part of it.

Man and horses against the miles! With time ever crowding at their shoulders, and raw danger always spurring beside them. The Pony Express. Ten days from San Francisco, far over at the edge of the western sea, to St. Joe, Missouri, half a continent away. Ten short days, because of flashing, speeding hoofs, with lean and purposeful men to ride above them. And it was around these reckless, speeding riders that all the rest of it was bound. All these plodding supply wagons, all the faithful keepers of the way stations along the far trails. So many and so much dedicated to one common purpose—that the express go through! And it was the rider and his horse that were the pulse beat, the throbbing heart of the whole enterprise.

Even the bearded man at the desk leaned back from his work

and listened, a spark lighting up his tired eyes. For this was Alex Majors, one of the three men who had conceived this whole thing, who had built it and made it work.

That distant echo hardened and became the mutter of speeding hoofs, and the clatter of these grew to a peak and came to a trampling halt outside the door. There was the mutter of a brief word or two, the slap of the leather mochila being swung from one saddle to another, then fresh hoofs exploding into action and beating out a rataplan of sound that dwindled and faded swiftly into the long distance.

A rider, gray with dust but still moving jauntily, came into the room. "Haslam reporting, Mister Majors."

The bearded man nodded. "And right on time, Bob. How are things across the desert?"

"Quiet enough between here and Shell Crossing. But the Goshiutes are stirring some around Egan Cañon. And Sam Keetley had a little brush with some White Knives at Rosebud Pass station. Feeling seems to be that the Indians are getting a little bolder all the time. If the military would do more scouting and less drilling, it would help."

Alex Majors shrugged, smiled faintly. "The military will always be the military, Bob. They have their own way of doing things. They'll move when they get ready."

The rider went out and now Alex Majors laid a direct glance on Clay Roswell. "You're probably waiting to see me?"

"Yes, sir." Roswell stepped over to the desk. "My name is Clay Roswell. I'd like to know if there's any chance of getting on with you as an express rider, Mister Majors?"

Alex Majors leaned back in his chair, pulled a black cheroot from a pocket, scratched a match, and lighted up. He looked at Roswell through a drift of smoke.

"Son, I could muster the equal of a cavalry troop from the waiting list ahead of you. You're a full year too late."

Roswell stood quietly for a moment, his thoughts flashing back in dark retrospect. "I was afraid that would be the answer," he said slowly. "A year ago was when I'd hoped to ask. Well, it's water under the bridge now. Thanks just the same, sir."

Alex Majors was a kindly man. His glance touched the faded, threadbare, almost ragged condition of Roswell's clothes.

"If you're up against it, son, perhaps we could find something for you to do around the corrals. But even that kind of a job can't last very long. You see, in about six months from now the Pony Express will be just a memory."

Roswell's head came up, surprise on his face. "A memory? I don't understand, sir."

"It's like this," said Alex Majors. "Within the next week or two the California State Company proposes to start the building of their new telegraph line. Work will start from this end and from Salt Lake simultaneously. When they meet, out in the desert somewhere, it means a tie-in all the way to Saint Joe, for the eastern stretch of the telegraph is already pretty much finished. And the day those two lines tie in, then the Pony Express is all through."

"Now I heard some talk of such a thing along the back trail," admitted Roswell slowly. "But nobody seemed to take much stock in it . . . seemed to feel it was just another wild rumor. There's always a lot of wild talk of this and that going on, sir. Do you really think they can build such a line? It's big country, and mighty wild and rough, between here and Salt Lake."

"They'll build it all right," said Alex Majors decisively. "Oh, they'll have their troubles, of course, just as we've had, not only in setting up our project, but in keeping it operating. There'll be all the natural hazards, plus the Indians. That means fighting, dead men, way stations raided, poles pulled down, wires cut . . . all that sort of thing. But in the end, son, the job will be done and kept done. They've got Jack Casement handling things at this end and he's a good man, one of the best. Tough, stubborn, smart, and two-fisted. The kind who won't lick easy."

Alex Majors freshened his cheroot with another match, gave Clay Roswell another careful looking over, then went on.

"I understand that Casement is looking for men, the smart, able, and dependable kind. Now, if I were young again, son, and wanted to have a hand in doing something big, in a big way, I'd go look up Jack Casement, have a talk with him, and see what he has to offer. Fine opportunity there."

For so long had Clay Roswell thought of the Pony Express as being something far too full of color and romance ever to die, it was a disturbing thing to hear a man like Alex Majors say flatly that its days were numbered. So Roswell came back to that fact.

"That's mighty tough about the Express, Mister Majors. There was never anything like it before, there'll never be anything like it again."

Alex Majors shrugged, spread his hands. "It's a changing world and a fast-moving one, son. We've had our day, served our purpose. There's no profit in moaning against progress. The world moves and men and their plans must move with it. I try and be a realist about such things. But they'll remember us . . . they'll always remember us. And what more can any man ask than a chance to carve a small, but lasting niche in history for himself and his work?"

For a short moment, Alex Majors mused over this thought, then shook himself, and bent again to the work on his desk.

"You go look up Jack Casement, son. I'm sure he'll have something for you. You'll most likely find him at the Shoshone Bar at this hour. That's where most of the important business of this post is talked over and settled. Good luck."

15

CHAPTER TWO

Fort Churchill, Nevada Territory in a July twilight of the year of 1861. Fogged with dust, feverish with activity, electric with vision and purpose. Crowded with people and wagons. Life at a hard, rumbling boil. Clay Roswell would have been something less than human if he'd remained untouched by the spirit of this frontier, by its ferocious activity. Things daring and tremendous were in the air, things already done and things yet to do, great new ventures in the march of empire, and all men seemed more or less drunk with the promise of them.

Dusk was steadily thickening and lights began coming on all across the town, throwing thin, dust-fogged gleams from door and window. Ahead loomed a big, square building, the double doors of which stood open, letting out a gush of amber light and through which men moved in and out of the place in a steady drift. Painted at a slant across a single long window and outlined against the light within were the words: *Shoshone Bar.*

Breasting the tide of men, Roswell worked his way through that busy doorway, stepping into a long rectangle of a room with a bar running the full length of one side, where men were jammed shoulder to shoulder and where three sweating bartenders tried to keep up with the demanding clamor. The balance of the place was taken up with gaming tables, each with men sitting around them, while other men, waiting for a chair to empty, milled back and forth.

Roswell wondered how he was going to locate this man, Jack

Casement, in all this jamming confusion, if indeed Casement was here. His best bet, he decided, was to ask one of the bartenders, for if Casement was as important in the scheme of things to come as Alex Majors had said he was, and if he frequented this place regularly, then the men behind the bar would probably know him.

As he began elbowing his way toward the bar, Roswell used the full advantage of his lean height to send his glance around the room, running it along the swarming bar, then out across the various little groups seated at the tables. His searching survey touched a table in a far corner, moved past it, then came swiftly back. He rocked up on his toes for a better look, while a ripple of feeling went across his face, turning it bleak. The gray of his eyes went dark, chilling.

It just couldn't be, he told himself. The favors of luck never fell that way to any man. What with all the wide wilderness of this frontier for them to be lost in, it seemed beyond belief that he'd find the Pickards right here in this room—right over there before his very eyes. Yet, of the four men sitting around that corner table, there was a bulk and burliness about two of them that took him far back to a lonely night camp along a distant trail, when treachery of the lowest kind had struck, when death had hovered close in the surrounding shadows.

Roswell began driving his way toward that corner table, swinging the weight of his shoulders from side to side, knocking men out of his way, paying no attention at all to their angry protests. A raw-boned teamster caught at him.

"Friend, the whole damned room don't belong to you!"

Roswell gave no heed to either the grip or the words, jerking loose and driving on, his every thought centered on that corner table and the men sitting around it.

Of the four at the table, one was of medium size, though compactly built, with square-cut features and a solid jaw, and

17

with blue eyes that seemed to blaze with a vast drive of inner energy. His hair was of a vigorous, ruddy shade, just off red. The man beside him was long-jawed, with intense and restless black eyes, a man big of limb and heavy through the shoulders. But as far as Clay Roswell was concerned, these two did not exist. It was the other pair with whom he was wholly concerned.

He broke into a slight clearing beside the table. The four men, engrossed in their talk, showed no interest in him, so Roswell, shifting a little to one side, had his good, fair look and knew now beyond all doubt that he had not been mistaken. Here were the Pickards, sure enough. Jess and Hoke Pickard.

The fury rolled up inside of Roswell, a fury that was cold and bitter. So many times during the long, thwarted months of the past year had he dreamed of such a meeting and of what he would do if fortune should ever be kind enough to bring it about. Well, fortune had smiled at last and there they were, right in front of him. Jess and Hoke Pickard. A bleak frenzy gripped him, calling on him to smash and destroy and kill.

If he'd had a gun, he'd have used it then and there, turned it loose without warning. But he had no weapon. He had nothing but his bare hands. Well, that wasn't going to hold him back, either that or anything else. Nothing mattered now—odds, weapons—nothing!

He grabbed the back of Jess Pickard's chair, hauled it and the man in it back from the table, and spun them around. Jess Pickard stared up at him, an oath of surprise breaking from his lips.

"Just what in hell . . . ?"

"Have a look, Pickard," rapped Roswell. "Have a good look! Now you must remember me?"

Jess Pickard, still in the grip of that surprise that comes before full anger, still staring, cursed again and growled.

"No, I don't remember you. But if you don't quit yanking

this chair and bothering me, I'll give you something that you'll damn' well remember as long as you. . . ."

"That's just it, Pickard," cut in Roswell. "You gave me something to remember once before. This is part of it." Roswell touched the scar above his temple. "Just about a year ago, it was. At a night camp in Weber Cañon, over past Salt Lake. Now you must remember that. Or do you so easily forget all the men you beat and rob and leave for dead? Ah! So you do remember . . . !"

Roswell saw the light of recognition flare up in Jess Pickard's eyes, a look almost of incredulity at first, such as a man might show on seeing a ghost. Then hard desperation flared in Jess Pickard. He came lunging up, throwing a warning at his brother.

"Hoke . . . look out!"

Roswell put all he had behind the fist that drove into Jess Pickard's face. All his weight, all the cold frenzy that was in him. Behind the punch was a year of brooding, of bitter, backed-up longing for elemental justice. And it added up to enough to hang Jess Pickard half-stunned and floundering across the back of his chair. For a moment he stayed there, and then, as Roswell hit him again, he slid off the chair and rolled on the floor. Roswell moved around to follow up.

It came near being a fatal move for him. For now Hoke Pickard came away from the table with a hard lunge, driving a slashing hand ahead of him. Naked steel gleamed in the yellow lamplight.

Roswell glimpsed the knife, swung out a warding left arm. He managed to keep the steel away from his body, but the burn of its thirsting edge ran hot across his forearm. He kicked savagely at Hoke's body, then whirled into the clear.

The kick had not landed squarely, so was only partially effective. It dropped Hoke to his knees, but did not disable him as Roswell had intended it should. Hoke hung onto his knife and now, dragging in a hoarse gasp of breath, surged to his feet again, shoulders low, hunched, his knife cutting flashing arcs of light back and forth in front of him as he weaved, feinting for an opening.

Clay Roswell grabbed the chair he'd knocked Jess Pickard out of, swung it high, and stepped in to meet Hoke and his knife just as Hoke made his second lunge, bringing the steel around in a curving upward drive, aiming for Roswell's stomach. Roswell brought the chair over and down with a savage, full-armed sweep.

The impact was vicious. The legs of the chair crumpled like matches, splintering across Hoke's head and shoulders. But the edge of the seat, solid and wicked, drove viciously home to Hoke's forehead, just below the hairline. Hoke went down soddenly, crumpled and without motion.

When the first blaze of trouble broke, the other two men at the table stayed in their chairs for a moment, startled and still. Then they came to their feet and the big man with the black eyes made as though to move in. But the ruddy-haired man pulled him back and spoke sharply to him. After that the ruddy-haired one watched closely, murmuring an instinctive protest when Hoke Pickard pulled his knife. And when Clay Roswell disposed of Hoke with that crashing chair, a gleam of approval shone in the ruddy-haired man's eyes. Now, surprisingly, he called a word of warning to Roswell.

"Watch the first one, lad!"

Jess Pickard needed watching. He was back on his feet again and he came in now with a headlong rush. He smashed into Roswell, grabbed him around the waist, and started driving him back in short, stiff-legged, jumping rushes, trying to corner him against the wall. Roswell, his arms free, beat down at the back of Jess's neck, clubbing him again and again at the base of the skull. This punishment was too much for Jess Pickard and his grip loosened, and Roswell spun free. With hoarse and gulping words he taunted Pickard.

"Different here than in Weber Cañon, eh, Pickard? You caught me in my blankets there, clubbed me, thought you'd cave my head in . . . and meant to. Well, try it now . . . try it now!"

Jess Pickard did, with another rush, which drove Roswell across the room, slamming into tables, sending chairs skidding wildly. Men scattered before them and Roswell finally brought up against the bar, and Jess Pickard held him there and belted him twice in the face with heavy, pawing blows that cut and bruised and hurt a man clear to the spine. For a moment the room whirled and pitched before Roswell's dazed eyes.

Pickard sensed his advantage and, had he been cooler-headed, might have finished things right then by stepping back and measuring his man. But Pickard was like a maddened animal now and he fought like one. He mauled and clawed and bulled at Roswell, trying to wrestle him off his feet. But the pressure of the bar at Roswell's back held him up.

Cold and bitter purpose had carried Clay Roswell this far in the affair and that purpose had been changing to black battle fury as the fight progressed. In that fury, Roswell found another reservoir of strength. His mouth set in a twisted, bloody snarl.

He brought both hands up, jammed the heels of them under Jess Pickard's jaw and, with a wicked surge of lifting power, snapped Pickard's head up and far back. A strangled bawl broke from Pickard and he gave ground. Roswell drove him savagely back, and, crashing into a table, they both fell over this and went rolling to the floor, the force of the fall breaking all grips.

Roswell got his hands and knees under him and stumbled to his feet. He thought he did it swiftly, but to the avid, watching circle of spectators it was a slow and lunging effort. Even so, he was up ahead of Jess Pickard and he sighted on Pickard's rising head and hammered his right fist home three times to Pickard's temple.

The first blow stopped Pickard's attempt to get up. The second started him back to the floor. The third sent him all the way there, where he lay, sodden and helpless.

Roswell shuffled back a couple of steps and stood with spread feet, bent slightly forward from the waist. Breath labored in and out of his lungs in hoarse gulps and his throat was slimed with a raw, harsh saltiness. The pulse of terrific and sustained effort thundered in his ears and his eyes felt hard and congested. For a long moment he stared down at his man. Then he began to mumble thickly, and only those close to him caught any part of the words.

"Now, I'll fix you . . . like you tried to fix me . . . beat your damned head in . . . beat it in."

He shuffled over to a chair, swung it high, moved back on Jess Pickard, held in a sort of deadly concentration. But then men moved in, got hold of him, took the chair away from him. One of them spoke, almost pleasantly.

"Enough's enough, lad. Murder's an ugly thing. You've whipped them. Let it stop here."

Roswell tried to pull free, raging at them thickly. There were too many of them. And that same pleasant voice kept saying: "Easy, lad . . . easy. The thing's done."

Finally he quieted. He scrubbed a hand across his eyes, his head lifted, and he came around to face the room of crowded watchers, who accorded him a voiceless tribute to a first-class fighting man. No explanation was asked of him and he offered none. He started for the door, still none too steady on his feet.

In the ruckus he'd lost his hat, but someone retrieved it and handed it to him. This was the ruddy-haired man who had been sitting at the table with the Pickards. Not only did the man return Roswell's hat, but he took him by the arm and moved with him to the door. Roswell, still all a-jump inside with the fever of combat, would have pulled free, but the man's grip tightened. And once more came that pleasant voice.

"Easy, lad. I'd be your friend. Where that fellow put his knife into your arm, you're leaking gore like a wounded buffalo. The arm needs looking after. I'm taking you where something can be done about it."

"Why should you give a damn?" demanded Roswell hoarsely. "Who are you?"

"I'm interested because I like your style and I like the fight in you," came the cheerful answer. "I'm looking for men who can handle themselves like you can. Me, I'm Jack Casement."

CHAPTER THREE

The cabin stood somewhat apart from the seething center of Fort Churchill. It glowed with light and the moment Clay Roswell stepped through the door the atmosphere of comfortable living enfolded him. The air was savory with the odors of warm food. From a rear room a clear voice called: "That you, Dad?"

"Right, Kitts," answered Jack Casement. "With a friend. Bring a basin of hot water, some towels, and some cloth for a bandage."

Casement dragged up a chair. "Take it easy, lad," he told Roswell. "We'll soon have that arm snugged up."

Roswell dropped into the chair thankfully, amazed how wobbly he felt and knowing a certain impatience with himself because of it. Jack Casement produced a flask. "Take a good drag," he advised. "It'll tie you together."

The liquor took hold immediately, wiping out the hollow gulf that lay under Roswell's short ribs. The dullness that had blunted his sensibilities began to lift. He said: "This is a lot of bother to you."

Casement merely grunted and began peeling back the sleeve of the wounded arm.

Heels tapped briskly and a girl came in from the rear room, carrying a steaming basin, some towels and cloth, and her words came on ahead of her.

"What kind of casualty have you dragged home this time,

Dad? You never will. . . ." She broke off, her eyes widening. Then she exclaimed: "Why, it's you . . . !"

Roswell stirred, but said nothing. Jack Casement's head came up. "What's this . . . what's this? Kitts, that sounded like you'd met this fellow before?"

The girl, recovering from her start of surprise, nodded. "I have. That pole that fell off a wagon and broke Dan Stock's leg? Well, I was in the way of it, too. This man got me clear. For thanks, I slapped his face. Of course, I didn't understand at the moment why he . . . he. . . ." She broke off, flushing a little.

Roswell squirmed, from embarrassment as well as from the bite of hot water on the knife wound. "Just happened to be handy," he muttered.

"Be damned!" said Jack Casement. "They told me about Dan Stock, but nobody said anything about you being around, Kitts. You mean that pole which crippled Stock might have hit you, too?"

"Not might, Dad. It surely would have, but for him."

"Well now," said Casement tersely, bending to work on the wound again. "They're adding up. The qualifications, I mean."

The girl looked at Casement keenly. "Qualifications? What are you talking about?"

Casement grinned. "This and that. Maybe I was thinking out loud, Kitts."

Surprisingly deft at this sort of thing, Casement soon had the wound cleaned and bandaged. The snug press of the bandage was a definite comfort. Casement said: "That does it. Like another pull at the flask, lad?"

Roswell shook his head. "Thanks. Maybe I better tag myself. The name is Clay Roswell."

Casement nodded. "This is my daughter, Katherine." He added, twinkling: "So she slapped your face, eh, lad? Well, she always did have a temper."

The girl flushed again. "Now, Dad. . . ."

Came a knock at the cabin door and a call. "Reed Owen, folks!

The girl turned quickly and her summons was clear. "Come on in, Reed."

It was the big man with the long jaw and restless black eyes who had been at the table with Casement and the Pickards in the Shoshone Bar. He closed the door and put his back to it. His glance sought the girl and he smiled.

"Just the way I like you best, Kitts. All crisp and neat in gingham and fresh from the kitchen."

The girl tossed her head, but her eyes smiled back at him. "Now if that isn't a man for you. Using that kind of blarney to angle for an invitation to supper. Well, you're invited, Reed."

The big man looked at Roswell. "Had a hunch this was where you'd bring him, Jack. Your business, of course, but why all the interest? Jess and Hoke Pickard are the ones who could really stand a little of this kind of care. Me, I'm trying to figure out why you sided against them?"

"I didn't side against them," said Casement. "I just got interested in Roswell, here. I sort of took a liking to his style."

"Meaning that you didn't like that of the Pickards?"

Casement shrugged, his words running a trifle blunt. "Long as you ask, no, I didn't. It was your idea, remember, that we hire them on. I told you I was willing to have a talk with them, which I did. I didn't promise anything beyond that. From the first I wasn't too much impressed. Then, after the fireworks, I was certain I didn't want them, while I did want this man here. Meet him. Clay Roswell. This is Reed Owen, my supply boss, Roswell. If what I hope is true . . . which is that you're open to taking on a job with me . . . you'll be working with him a lot."

Reed Owen acknowledged the introduction with a brief nod. "Nothing personal in this, you understand. But, Jack . . . what do you know about this fellow? You never laid eyes on him up to half an hour ago. And when you did, the circumstances were a little surprising, to say the least. He came barging in out of nowhere and, without warning or any apparent reason, tried to beat the brains out of a couple of good men with a chair. That the kind of recommendation you like, Jack?"

"In this case, yes," answered Casement dryly. "I just got a feeling in this matter, Reed. As for me knowing anything about Roswell, what do you know about the Pickards? They've been working for you about a month, hauling poles down out of the mountains. Beyond that, what? Hell, man, there's precious little we know about any of those we hire. Out in country like this, men are a long ways away from the past years of their lives. About all we have to go on is just an instinct in such matters."

Clay Roswell got to his feet. "I seem to be the center of something here, so maybe I better have my own say. It happens, Mister Casement, that I would like to land a job with you. That was why I went into the Shoshone Bar in the first place. I was looking for you. Alex Majors of the Pony Express told me you were looking for men, and that I might locate you in the Shoshone Bar. The fact that I happened to run across the Pickards at the same table with you was just one of those things. Now, I still want that job. But we can talk that over tomorrow. I've been enough trouble to you for one day. And thanks a lot for taking care of this arm for me."

Casement said: "Son, you're not getting away from me. You're staying right here and eating supper with us. Tomorrow I'll probably have plenty for you to do besides talking. Just now you could stand a little more cleaning up. Go on into the kitchen. Kitts will round up a basin and some more hot water."

Reed Owen said: "Jack, don't you think you ought to find out a little more . . . ?"

"All in good time," cut in Casement bluntly. "Go ahead,

Roswell. Kitts, give the lad a hand."

Roswell hesitated, then shrugged and went into that back room. Katherine Casement followed him, filled the basin with hot water, put it on a bench in the corner. Then she watched while Roswell, working a little awkwardly with only one hand, washed the dust and grime and blood from his face, flinching slightly as he covered places where Jess Pickard's mauling fists had landed. Using the towel the girl handed him, he grinned crookedly.

"You're looking at the horrible example of what can come out of a saloon brawl, Miss Casement."

She surveyed him in grave silence. Her coppery hair glowed, thick and rich, under the lamplight. She had her father's intense blue eyes and her mouth was softly scarlet above a well-formed and decisive chin. Her skin was flawless, warmly sun-tanned.

"Saloon brawls," she said crisply, "never improved any man. Would you say you were better off for the one you were in?"

Roswell considered gravely, then nodded. "That's a good question. And, though it may sound strange to you, yes, I am better off. I feel that I'm a whole man again. You see, Miss Casement, if a man carries a thirst for vengeance long enough without slaking it, he can turn sour. He becomes prisoner to his own venom. Now I feel I'm a free man once more."

She studied him a little more carefully, as though seeing more to him than she first perceived. "You don't speak like a barbarian, but your acts and what Reed Owen said suggests a streak of it in you."

"A lot that Reed Owen doesn't know about it," Roswell said dryly. "But for that matter there's some barbarian in most men if you dig deep enough for it."

Her manner softened a little. "I'm not acting very generous, am I? After all, you did save me from being broken up by that pole, so I should be thanking you instead of criticizing you. I'm sorry I slapped you. But for a moment I thought. . . ." She broke off, soft color washing through her face.

"Sure," said Roswell easily, "I know. You thought a wild man from the desert had you." He grinned. "I've got to admit you swing a lusty slap. My head really buzzed."

Her flush deepened and she turned back to the stove.

Jack Casement and Reed Owen came in and took places at the table. Clay Roswell sat across from Kate Casement. The food was good and plentiful and there was raw hunger in Roswell. He ate silently, measuring the feeling about the table.

Two things he was quickly aware of. As yet, there was no great friendliness in Reed Owen toward him. But there definitely was a friendship between Owen and Kate Casement, perhaps even a deeper feeling. Owen sat at the girl's left and there was a certain intimacy in their traded glances and murmured words.

Jack Casement ate with the complete absorption of a hungry man and his plate was practically clean before he leaned back and bent a shrewd and suddenly coldly penetrating glance on Roswell.

"All right, lad," he said abruptly. "Now we must know about several things. When Reed here said that you came down out of nowhere and started trouble in the Shoshone Bar without apparent cause or reason, he told it as it certainly must have looked to a lot of men. Yet, while you were working out on that fellow, Jess Pickard, you also laid a few remarks on him. Enough to give me a hint as to why you tied into him and his brother the way you did. You say you'd like to go to work for me. Whether you do or not, depends on the rest of the story . . . all of it. I'm listening."

Roswell sat quietly for a time, his face pulling bleak with the memory. Then he began.

"When word of the Pony Express being formed reached Texas, I was hit with the idea of getting a job with them riding express. So I came up across the Strip and into Kansas. At a way station there I was told that the best chance of landing such a job was out here along the desert stretch, so I headed here. I had a fair stake of money and a pretty good outfit. Along the trail I caught up with the Pickards, Jess and Hoke. They'd run into some hard luck, they said, lost their wagon and most of their grub and gear by a slide during a storm. Their horses weren't much, either. Anyway, I offered to see them through as far as Salt Lake.

"We made a camp one night in Weber Cañon, east of Salt Lake. It was a pretty wild night, stormy and black. And that night, while I was in my blankets, Jess and Hoke Pickard jumped me and set out to club me to death. They figured they'd done a job of it, too. Anyhow, they stole my stake of money, my horses and outfit, and left me there as dead."

Roswell's words ran out into a taut silence. He lifted an unconscious finger to that scar just inside the hairline above his temple. His eyes darkened with remembrance of that savage night. Jack Casement, listening intently, stirred a little and flashed a sardonic glance at Reed Owen.

"Nice playmates, the Pickards. Go on, lad."

"Not much else," continued Roswell. "An emigrant party coming through, found me still alive, and carried me with them as far as Salt Lake, where they left me in the care of the Mormons. I guess it was touch and go for a time, but those good people pulled me through. It was a long time though before I could start working my way West once more, doing odd jobs along the trail at the Pony Express way stations for my food and a place to sleep. It was a good life. It gave me back my full health. I never dreamed I'd run across the Pickards here in Fort Churchill within a couple of hours after I arrived. But I did, and, when I saw them there in the Shoshone Bar . . . well, something just seemed to explode in me and I went after them.

That's the story."

Jack Casement flashed another glance at Reed Owen. "Now what do you think of my judgment of men, Reed? You were sold on a pair of damned thieves. I like my choice better. I told you I had an instinct in such things."

Reed Owen shrugged. "You've heard Roswell's story. Maybe the Pickards could tell another one."

"Not to me, they can't," declared Casement. "When Roswell jumped them, it was one against two. Yet, what was the first thing Hoke Pickard did? He pulled a knife. Me, I don't like knife men. And whatever story the Pickards told, I wouldn't believe it. I like this lad's. It rings with truth. As far as the Pickards are concerned, as of now they're through with any part of this job . . . hauling poles or anything else. If they should be around tomorrow, you tell them that. I doubt they'll show, though. They'll probably be long gone, now that Roswell has caught up with them."

Reed Owen shrugged, slouched a little in his chair, said nothing.

Casement turned to Roswell. "What sort of work did you hope to get with me, lad?"

"I'll leave that up to you, sir," answered Roswell.

"You've had schooling?"

"Quite a bit," acknowledged Roswell. "I had an uncle who was a minister. While I was growing up, he kept my nose in books a great deal. At the time I couldn't see much sense to it, for as a kid I'd have much rather been out working cattle. As I grew older, however, I realized what a wise man my uncle was, and how much I owed him for the time and trouble he took with me."

"That cinches it," said Jack Casement. "Lad, how'd you like to be my wagon boss?"

Reed Owen jerked upright in his chair. "Wagon boss! Oh,

come now, Jack. Be serious. It's one thing to offer Roswell a job of sorts. But wagon boss is something else. You can't be thinking. . . ."

"Know what I want, Reed," cut in Casement. "And I am serious . . . plenty. I tell you I got a feeling about this. I believe I'm right. Well, lad . . . how about it?"

Clay Roswell was too completely stunned to answer for a moment. Things were just moving too fast. He finally got some words out. "That's a big order, Mister Casement. I'd be happy to work for you at any job, of course. But there's a lot I don't know about wagon work."

"Not afraid to tackle it, are you?" Casement was leaning forward now, the easy humor gone. His face was hard and the blaze in his blue eyes deepened once more. "You don't have to know much about the actual handling of wagons. I can round up plenty of plug teamsters who know how to load and drive a wagon, who know how to take care of their wagon and their teams, who can follow, but who can't lead. And I've got to have a man who can lead. I've got to have a man who can help me organize, who can understand not one wagon, but a hundred of them. A man who can go over waybills and invoices and supply lists and know what they mean without chewing his tongue hopelessly."

Casement got to his feet, took a couple of turns up and down the room. There was an explosive well of energy in this man that was like a wind-driven flame. He went on.

"I've got to have a man I can trust implicitly, who I can depend on as I would my own right hand. A man young enough to have daring and enthusiasm, yet old enough to know balance and judgment. A man who is a fighter and who won't lose his nerve when the going gets rough. For it will be, rough as hell. Those are the things I want in my wagon boss . . . all of them!"

He came to a stop beside Roswell, shot his first question

again. "Afraid to tackle it?"

Roswell stood up, facing him. "All these things you say you need in a wagon boss . . . do you see them in me?"

Their glances locked, held for a long moment. Then Casement answered crisply: "I'm offering you the job. And would I, otherwise?"

Clay Roswell drew a deep breath. "I'm your man. No, I'm not afraid to tackle it. And you'll have all of my best. Here's my hand on it, sir."

To Clay Roswell that hand grip put a seal on a great many things. Mainly a complete fidelity to the purposes and needs of this man before him, this man with the electric blue eyes, the tumultuous energy, who could be coldly harsh one moment and winningly gentle the next. Now came that warmth again, as Jack Casement smiled.

"Good lad . . . good lad! I say again, I have a feeling about this. Neither of us will regret it. Now there are things to do. I want to get down and see how Dan Stock is making out with that broken leg, and I want you to meet some of my other men, Clay. Think that arm will stand up to a fairly busy evening?"

"Of course, sir. Whatever you say."

They moved to the door. Reed Owen remained in his chair, frowning. Roswell looked past him at Katherine Casement. "My thanks for everything, Miss Casement. You've been very kind."

She met his glance and gave him a small, grave nod, which left him wondering whether it reflected approval or otherwise. And as suddenly as a strong, keen wind striking out of nowhere, it came to Clay Roswell that it could matter a great deal what this copper-haired daughter of Jack Casement really thought of him.

Chapter Four

The next few days were the busiest Clay Roswell had ever known. There were endless details to be grasped, absorbed, and translated into action. Jack Casement had told him that, while the date of the jump-off into the desert had already been tentatively set, the exact time must really be when all the needed wagons and the men to drive them had been organized and made ready to roll.

"We've the wagons and the animals," said Casement. "The right men to handle them is the main problem. There are smart men and fools, brave men and cowards. So we must winnow them out and, as far as possible, pick only the smart and the brave. For once we start, our wagons must be kept rolling . . . must be! Everything depends on our wagons and what they haul."

These words lived with Roswell. He drove himself mercilessly, even though his wounded arm left him feeling a trifle seedy for a time. He had one stroke of tremendous good luck. He bumped into Bill Yerkes, the grizzled teamster he'd ridden in with out of the desert. Yerkes had a split lip, a black eye, and a look of supreme satisfaction.

Roswell grinned. "Who was the other fellow, friend?"

Bill Yerkes spat. "Bucko Yoland, the dirty scut! Alex Majors's wagon boss. He's had it in for me for a long time, but he never tried to get too nasty while Majors was around. But Alex left yesterday for an inspection trip of the desert stations, and with him gone Yoland didn't waste any time starting to rawhide me around. Now I'm a man who can take a cussin'-out when I got it coming. But no man can blackguard me unfairly. I proved that to Mister Bucko Yoland the hard way." Bill rolled a cud of blackstrap carefully across a bruised mouth and spat again.

"That could mean that right now you're probably out of a job," said Roswell. "I hope so."

Yerkes cocked his grizzled head. "And why do you hope so?"

"Because I need a good man to help me handle Jack Casement's wagons. How about it, Bill? As my *segundo?*"

Yerkes tipped his hat over one eye, felt tenderly of a lump on the back of his head. "You tempt me, boy . . . you surely do." Then he grinned sheepishly. "Ah, I wouldn't try and fool you. I was out to look you up and see if you could use me. For I been hearing things about you that I liked. About you whaling the daylights out of them worthless Pickards, and that Casement had made you his wagon boss. So if you really mean what you just said, you've hired yourself a man."

Bill Yerkes proved to be invaluable. He knew the wagon trade from the ground up, he knew men, and he knew the desert and what it could hold. He had a wide circle of friends among those of his trade and he knew which had the stuff in them, and which did not. And with him advising here and suggesting there, Roswell was able to report all in readiness to Jack Casement, far more quickly than he'd dared hope.

Like Alex Majors of the Pony Express, Jack Casement had an office in a corner of a big warehouse. Stored in the warehouse and stacked all about the place were mountains of supplies. The gathering and replenishing of these was Reed Owen's job. He ran it with a heavy, but efficient hand. He was in Casement's office when Roswell went in to report and he turned to Roswell curtly.

"I've got my end of the job well in hand, Roswell. The sup-

plies are ready and waiting. When are you going to have those
wagons ready? Good days are slipping away from us."

Roswell eyed him levelly, wondering at the obvious dislike
and antagonism this man showed toward him. He gave back
curtness for curtness.

"The wagons are ready now."

Reed Owen's lip curled. "I don't mean just a few wagons. I
mean all of them."

"And that's what I mean," shot back Roswell. "All of them.
Wagons, men, and teams. Ready to roll the minute Mister Casement gives the word."

Jack Casement, listening at his desk, lifted a triumphant
eyebrow at Reed Owen. "Now, didn't I tell you that you were
yelling before you were hurt, Reed? Clay, that's good work."

Katherine Casement was sitting at her father's elbow, helping
him wade through a mountain of paperwork. Roswell was
conscious of her guarded glance. He'd drawn an advance against
his first month's wages and had outfitted himself from head to
foot in new clothes and he had the satisfaction of knowing he
could face this girl now without the uncomfortable feeling that
he was just a short jump above a rag picker. Besides the new
clothes there was a Dragoon revolver, holstered at his lean hips.
At this, Reed Owen directed a sarcastic remark.

"That gun must weigh you down, Roswell. Didn't know the
camp had grown that wild."

"The next time a man with a knife comes at me, I might not
have a saloon chair handy," Roswell drawled. "And it won't be
long before we're out in the desert."

"With an army of men," scoffed Owen.

Roswell shrugged. "Big place, the desert. Lots more to it than
meets the eye. I've had a good look at it. Evidently you haven't,
Owen." He turned to Casement. "When will you want the
wagons brought up for loading, sir?"

Casement leaned back in his chair, stared at the ceiling with narrowed, speculative eyes. "Never pays to make a jump until you got your feet set solid," he murmured. "But I'd say we're about as ready as we'll ever be. Tentative date for the jump-off was next Monday. But if we made it tomorrow, we'd be five days to the good. And somewhere out in the desert we'll probably be able to use those five days to good account. We'll do it!"

He hit his feet with a surge of that deep energy. "We'll load this afternoon and jump off tomorrow at dawn! Kitts, you'll have to do what you can with this cussed paperwork. I'm riding out to the survey camp, to see Tom Hughes, so he can light a fire under his boys. Reed, you get your warehouse gang organized for a heavy afternoon. Plenty for all of us to do. Let's get at it!"

CHAPTER FIVE

Loading began right after midday. Wagon after wagon pulled in at the supply yards and warehouse. Men sweated, swore, and toiled mightily, and, as soon as one loaded outfit creaked ponderously off, there was always an empty one to move into place. Clay Roswell sent Bill Yerkes to oversee the job at the main warehouse, while he himself watched and helped the work at the pole yard. Here men with pike pole and peavy, rope and tackle, chains and plain brute strength rolled and skidded and hauled poles into position on the wagons.

On taking over his job as wagon boss for Casement, Roswell had known only one slight uncertainty, and that was how he was going to be accepted by the men. They were a rough and hardy outfit, these wagon men of a wild frontier. Most of them were older men than Roswell, and he felt that it would have been only natural if some of them had been disgruntled over taking orders from a younger man, and one who was a comparative stranger. But he met up with surprisingly little argument, and he wondered about this.

Bill Yerkes could have explained it to him. Some of these men had seen that wild battle that had taken place in the Shoshone Bar. The rest had heard about it, and Roswell's part in it had not suffered any in the telling and retelling. He had been one man against two, one of these with a knife, and he had beaten them soundly. Also, the Pickards had achieved some reputation around Fort Churchill as being a mean and tough pair to tangle with.

It was a rough code these men toiling with the wagons and the loading of them lived by. In that code, a first-class fighting man rated high. In their eyes, Clay Roswell had more than qualified. So they respected him and, because of that, were cheerful at taking and obeying his orders. Also, they liked the way he gave those orders.

There was no shouting, cursing, or ranting. He spoke quietly and only when it was necessary, and they approved of this easy, taciturn manner. Where he could, and as much as his wounded arm would permit, Roswell lent his own strength to the job. Because of all these things, the men accepted him and, realizing it, Roswell knew a warm satisfaction and gave out his liking in return.

He had just checked over another loaded wagon, seen that the poles were all well-balanced and solidly in place and that the retaining chains were properly set, when Bill Yerkes sought him out. Bill's eyes were glinting angrily under bushy brows.

"You're needed over at the warehouse, lad. Trouble there."

Roswell looked at him, startled. "What kind of trouble, Bill?"

"That feller Owen. Who in hell does he think he is, anyhow? How much say has he got over us wagon men?"

"None that I know of. What's this all about?"

"Well, this Owen was out to overload Skip Keswick's wagon with flour, and, when Skip set out to argue with him about it, Owen hauled off and knocked Skip down, with Skip hardly more'n half his size. So now Skip is ready to quit and some of the other boys who saw the fracas are takin' the same frame of mind. It's an idea that could grow. The time to stop that sort of thing is right now and it looms up as your chore."

"That's right," said Roswell crisply. "We'll see about it"

Things had come to a dead halt at the loading platform of

the warehouse. A wagon stood beside the platform, stacked high with barreled flour. It took only a glance to see that it was loaded well beyond reasonable capacity. Some empty wagons stood farther back, with an uneasy crowd of teamsters grouped about them. One of the teamsters was a wiry little man, mopping at a bleeding mouth with a faded bandanna handkerchief. The men eyed Clay Roswell uneasily as he came up to them.

To the wiry little man, Bill Yerkes said: "Tell it again, Skip."

Skip Keswick told it, a hard anger in his voice. "That's my outfit yonder. It's loaded 'way past all common sense. Trying to buck the desert with that load would be just asking for a breakdown at the first stretch of rough going. Besides which, it'd kill off a string of mules inside the first ten miles."

The little teamster dabbed at his mouth again and went on. "All of which I tried to tell that god-damned Owen feller. He told me to shut up and get out of the way, that he was runnin' the loadin' job. I set to argue some more and he hauls off and knocks me down. Now if that's the way this deal is goin' to run, then Jack Casement can have his damned job. I'm going to quit you, Roswell."

Roswell dropped a hand on the little man's shoulder. "No you're not, Skip. You wait right here. I'm having a little talk with Owen!"

As Roswell headed over to the warehouse, Reed Owen and Katherine Casement came out on the platform. Owen was scowling. He shot heavy words at Roswell.

"Thought you claimed to have your wagon men in hand, Roswell? This don't look like it. Have them get that wagon out of the way and make room for another. Me and my men are anxious to get on with the loading chore."

Roswell put a hand on the platform, vaulted up onto it. He straightened and moved in on Reed Owen, stopping just one short stride away, a boring glance in his gray eyes that had gone dark and chill.

"Before we get at the rest of the matter, Owen," he said bleakly, "here is something I'm going to tell you just *once*. Just once so don't forget it. Don't you ever hit one of my men again! Now you ought to feel proud of yourself, taking a swing at Skip Keswick, with him not more than two-thirds your size. Must have taken a lot of nerve to do that. But listen close. Don't ever do it again. Any time you got a complaint to make against one of my teamsters, you come to me and let me straighten matters out. Do I make myself clear?"

That group of teamsters, edging in, heard every word of Roswell's flat declaration and their eyes gleamed their satisfaction.

Reed Owen rolled up on his toes. "Wish Jack Casement was here to listen to that kind of talk. He'd put you back into place in a hurry, Roswell. Long as he isn't, I'll handle that job myself. Now if you want some of the same that Keswick got, you can have it, right here and now."

This was as far as Reed Owen got before Katherine Casement was between the pair of them, putting Owen at her back and facing Roswell.

"Stop it, both of you! This is a fine affair, indeed. I'm sure Dad would approve of it . . . oh, very much. A nice way to start off an undertaking as big and important as this is. Stop this silly arguing, right now! Mister Roswell, we can't load any more wagons until this one is moved. Will you kindly attend to it?"

Roswell looked at her gravely. Her dander was up, plenty. Her eyes were full of sparks and spots of high color burned in her cheeks. Well, what he was going to tell her wouldn't soften the lightning any.

"Miss Casement, that wagon will be moved when the load has been cut down to a sane limit, with Skip Keswick, whose job it will be to drive the outfit, judging what the load limit will be." He looked past her at Reed Owen. "Cut that load down to proper size, Owen, or that wagon stays right there."

"Hell with you!" blurted Owen. "I've loaded plenty of wagons in my time. I know how much an outfit can carry. But a damn' lazy 'skinner would rather ride a light load than a heavy one. Easier for him. I'm telling you, Roswell, get somebody up there to move that wagon!"

"Not until the load is cut down to what it should be," returned Roswell flatly. "That stands."

Katherine Casement stamped an angry foot. "This is ridiculous! The idea that everything should come to a stop because of a silly argument between two . . . two . . . ! Can't you understand, Clay Roswell, that we're wasting valuable time and that Reed is responsible for moving our supplies? Can't . . . ?"

"And I'm responsible for the wagons that carry those supplies," broke in Roswell. "A broken-down wagon or a worked-out string of mules is my problem, not Owen's. As far as time is concerned, it's better to waste a little of it here, than a great deal out in the desert where a breakdown could be mighty serious." He turned, waved, and called: "Bill Yerkes, come here!"

Bill left the group of teamsters and came over.

"Bill," said Roswell, "you've been running freight outfits all your life. Will you please tell Miss Casement your opinion about this argument?"

Bill Yerkes touched his hat as he looked at the girl.

"Miss, I'm giving you the truth. That wagon is overloaded by a full half ton or better. Now I know what the desert is . . . I've been hauling across it steady for the Pony Express for the past year. It's rough and it's wild and it takes plenty out of a wagon and a team even under the best of conditions. Loaded the way it is, that wagon wouldn't last a day's travel. And that's the simple fact of it."

There was no guile in Bill Yerkes. But there was a rugged simplicity and truth that the girl could not ignore. She nibbled a red underlip, then shrugged.

"Very well. You should know what you're talking about. Reed, have your men cut the load down to what the teamsters think is right." With that, she turned and went into her father's office.

This was gall and wormwood to Reed Owen. He flushed with a dark and savage anger. He stared after Katherine Casement, then brought his fuming black eyes back to Clay Roswell, who smiled grimly.

"You've had your orders, Owen. And once more this warning. Don't use your fists on one of my men again. Try them on me."

Owen let out a low, furious curse. "That will probably come, Roswell."

Roswell nodded easily. "Beginning to think so myself. But right now the important thing is to get that load down to size."

Gray eyes locked with black ones and the black ones turned away. Reed Owen yelled harshly to his warehouse hands and barrels of flour began coming down off Skip Keswick's wagon. Roswell called the little teamster over.

"This better, Skip?"

Skip, moving with a little swagger, nodded. "I'll haul my share any time, any place. But I don't break down my wagon or kill off my team for any man. Obliged, boss."

Reed Owen turned and stamped into the gloom of the warehouse. Clay Roswell hesitated a moment, then went into Jack Casement's office. Katherine Casement was at the desk, busy with the mound of paperwork. Her coppery head came up with an antagonistic tilt.

"You should be supremely satisfied." She shrugged. "You won your point."

Roswell smiled gravely. "No. Common sense won the point.

But I wasn't thinking about that. I came in to tell you that I was sorry there was a fuss and to thank you for seeing the side of the wagon men."

"One side or the other had to concede the point, and there was a stubborn, pig-headed look about you which told me you never would. So. . . ." She shrugged slim shoulders.

Roswell's smile became a grin. "Wonder if it'll always be that way?"

She eyed him a trifle warily. "I don't know what you mean."

"My motives, and the way you misunderstand them. Anyhow, this time you didn't slap my face."

Color whipped her cheeks. "Maybe I'd have liked to. I can't stand stubborn, pig-headed men."

"Now I can't blame you there," he drawled. "Don't like the brutes myself. But anyhow . . . thanks."

He touched his hat and left.

Katherine Casement watched him go, a tall, solid-shouldered man who moved with a light, sure ease. There was, she realized, a boyish humor in this man, but there was also a core of hard, tough maturity that leaped from his gray eyes when they darkened and turned cold.

Twice she had seen that look show. The first time had been just the briefest flash, before humor wiped it out. That was when she had slapped him, after the episode of the rolling log. The second time had been just a few moments ago, when he faced Reed Owen out on the warehouse platform. She weighed the judgment her father had shown in picking Clay Roswell as his wagon boss, and she had to admit that so far the choice had been a good one.

From the night her father had first brought Roswell into the cabin, a ragged, bruised, and bloody figure, and, after hearing Roswell's own account of the background of his feud with the Pickards, Kate Casement had known increasing curiosity concerning all the details of that fight in the Shoshone Bar. She had shied away from asking her father about it, but from a warehouse hand who had seen the battle she had got the full picture. And though she found it a little difficult to visualize the lean, brown, quietly smiling man who had just faced her, as the berserk, savage destroyer that the warehouse hand pictured, it was obvious that when fully aroused Clay Roswell could be a wicked fighting man.

She recalled again the picture of Roswell and Reed Owen facing each other out there on the platform, and she stirred uneasily at what it foretold. Something lay between these two men, some rough edge of antagonism. She knew of no good cause for this. She'd heard that it was that way sometimes between two men. They met, they looked into each other's eyes, and they hated, then and from then on. Something in their natures, some alien and opposing elements in the physical chemistry of their make-ups, doomed them to an inevitable clash. Between these two, that clash was something which had to be definitely headed off, for the good of all and for that of the big job ahead. Kate made a mental note to speak to her father about it.

With the atmosphere cleared, things moved along rapidly at the warehouse. Wagons rumbled up, were loaded, rumbled away. No further argument arose over how much a wagon could take. When the teamster of that wagon said enough, that was it. In the office, Kate Casement was able to get well along with her paperwork. And then it was Reed Owen who came in and dropped into a chair.

"Sorry, Kitts," he said. "About getting rough out there a while ago. But that fellow Roswell gets under my skin. I don't like the way he throws his weight around. Wish I could feel as sure of him as your father does."

The girl eyed him with a severity she did not altogether feel.

She liked Reed Owen a lot. They had been thrown much together since they first met a year previous, over in Sacramento, across the Sierra Nevada Mountains to the west. Which was when her father had been selected to be in charge of the western desert and of construction of the proposed line between Fort Churchill and Salt Lake.

Reed Owen, she realized, had his faults. But what man was without them? There was a rough streak in him when his temper was aroused. He was restless and aggressive and could be overly swift in his judgment at times. But there was also a broad streak of charm in the man when he wanted to turn it on.

"I really am a little disappointed in you, Reed," she told him. "Particularly over your striking that little teamster. That wasn't exactly a brave gesture."

Reed Owen squirmed. "I know it, and I'm sorry about it, now. This damned temper of mine. . . . It always does get me into trouble. I hope someday to learn to control it. I say again . . . I'm sorry."

She relented and smiled. "Sometimes grown men can be ridiculously like pugnacious small boys. About Clay Roswell . . . well, there seems to be no accounting for likes and dislikes, Reed. Some men seem fated to clash. Perhaps that's the way it is between you and Roswell. But for the good of all concerned I do hope you'll try and avoid any more arguments. After all, Clay Roswell is Dad's man, and one of the team."

"I know," Owen admitted. "But for some reason he sure gets my roach up. Just so you're not mad at me, I'll try and get along with the devil himself."

Her smile grew warmer. "Spoken like a little gentleman, Reed. Now there's still a lot of work to do. Let's get at it."

The afternoon wore along and ran out. The sun dipped from sight beyond the distant blue rampart of the world that was the Sierras. At the military post the bugles sang and the flag floated earthward. Fort Churchill, the town, seethed and rumbled and smoked with dust.

Clay Roswell and Bill Yerkes moved about among the loaded wagons drawn up in orderly lines, all set for the charge into the desert at tomorrow's dawn. Teamsters who had placed their loaded wagons, and then put their teams away in the corrals, now were back, checking their wagons again, making sure that all was ready, that dust tarpaulins were snug and securely lashed, that grease was where grease was needed, and that harness and other such gear was in top shape.

The excitement of the thing was getting hold of even the stodgiest now. It was, thought Clay Roswell, always that way with any big job that was also an adventure. There was always a period of waiting around, of preparation, during which some men were bound to slack off through sheer boredom. But once the actual moment of starting was set and close at hand, then the spirit of the thing revived and gripped all men.

Satisfied that everything was as ready as it was possible to make it, Roswell turned to Bill Yerkes and voiced a final thought. "I'm wondering if it might not be smart to put a guard on the wagon camp for the night, Bill?"

"Well, now," answered Yerkes, "I was wonderin' if you'd get around to thinking that, son. And I say, yes! Because, while there's a heap of stuff on some of these wagons that's valuable to the job but nobody else, there's also some other loads that would be almost like pure gold to any jackleg who might get his hands on it. For instance, that load of flour yonder. Some things are in mighty short supply on this side of the mountains, and flour is one of them. Well, mebbe flour ain't exactly worth its weight in gold, but it is worth enough to cause some maverick to lift a couple of barrels of it, should he get half a chance. And this part of the country has got its share of such mavericks. So I think puttin' on a guard for the night would be right smart business."

"Then we'll do it." Roswell nodded. "I'll stand a shift myself."

"No, you won't," declared Yerkes. "Some jobs the boss don't do. You leave this to me, boy. I'll pick a couple of good men."

Bill Yerkes hurried away to tend to this angle and Roswell, realizing that after the jump-off it could be quite some time before he'd have the chance again, headed into town to a supply post to pick up a few more items of personal gear and extra clothes.

In the trading post a gaunt emigrant was dickering with a clerk. "Your prices are pretty steep, mister, but not too much out of line, all things considered. It's them damn' little posts along the trail that rob a man. Me and the old lady and the kids come on in from Myers Wells on damn' short rations, rather than pay the robber prices they're askin' out there."

The clerk shrugged. "You better stock up plenty before startin' over the mountains, friend. If you think they're tough at Myers Wells, just try them at Sugar Pine or Bear Wallow. Prices there will really make you scream."

By the time Roswell had bought what he wanted and got back on the streets again, it was full dark, with lights winking yellow through the dust. Two men moved into a pool of light on the far side of the street. Recognition was instant with Roswell. The Pickards, Jess and Hoke.

The old, cold fury rushed up in Roswell again, urging him to go after them. He'd manhandled them once, but that was only part of the pay-off. He was halfway across the street before the realization hit him that this wouldn't do. For he was no longer a jobless drifter, owning nothing but a black thirst for vengeance. He was a part of a big and epic undertaking, carrying the trust and confidence and authority that Jack Casement had bestowed upon him.

What would happen if he went after the Pickards again? At

best just another savage brawl, which would prove nothing that had not already been established. And even if he were lucky enough and good enough to beat them down again, it could settle nothing, or bring anything back. And this time he might not be that good or that lucky. This time maybe Hoke's knife would get home where it really counted, or maybe there might be a gun on Jess. And then, where the big job, the great adventure?

He came to a halt, shaking his head. Hell with the Pickards! He'd beaten them, whipped them, left his mark on them. They didn't count any more.

He stared after the Pickards and a big man joined them, just before they moved on out of the light, to be swallowed up in the dark, shifting mass of the crowd. The man was Reed Owen. Moving on about his own business, Roswell wondered about this.

It was a full hour later that Clay Roswell knocked at the door of the Casement cabin, then went on in at Casement's yelled summons. Jack Casement was at the supper table, just in from his trip out into the desert. Also at the table were Katherine Casement and Reed Owen. Casement waved a welcoming hand.

"Pull up a chair and dig in, Clay. How are those wagons?"

"Loaded and ready to roll. Thanks, but I've had supper. I just dropped around to see if there were any final instructions."

"No change. We roll at dawn." Casement smiled. "Pawing the ground to get going, eh, lad?"

"It'll be good to get at the main job," Roswell admitted. "See you in the morning."

"Don't rush off," admonished Casement. "Come to think of it, there is something I want to talk to you about."

Roswell took a chair, waited quietly. He glanced at Katherine Casement, but she avoided his eyes. He looked at Reed Owen and saw the same old antagonism flare in Owen's eyes; also, there was something that looked like a gleam of mockery. Roswell's own expression became taciturn, inscrutable. It wasn't hard to guess what it was Casement wished to talk about.

Casement downed a final mouthful of coffee, pushed back from the table, and swung around in his chair. "Tomorrow," he said bluntly, "we tackle a big job. I shouldn't have to explain how important that job is, not only to me and the company behind me, but to this entire nation. It's going to take the best of every one of us to put it across. Once we start, there'll be neither time nor place for any sort of quarreling among ourselves. I want that thoroughly understood. Clay, I understand that you and Reed, there, did a bit of bristling at each other this afternoon. I want no more of it."

Casement's electric blue eyes burned at Roswell. There was a shadow in Roswell's glance as he met Casement's look and held it. "You've told Owen the same, sir?" he asked quietly.

"I've told him."

"And you've heard the cause of the argument?"

Casement waved an impatient hand. "Enough of it. If any two men in the organization should co-operate, it's you two. Reed running his supply end, and you the wagons."

"That," said Roswell softly, "will suit me just fine. So long as he runs his warehouse and doesn't try and tell my teamsters what to do, even if he has to use his fists on them."

"What's that?" Casement jerked up a trifle straighter.

Roswell smiled, a little crookedly and without mirth. "That's the rest of the story, sir. Everything will be ready at dawn."

This time Roswell was out of the house before Casement could call him back.

There was a strange and brittle anger in him. Not because of anything Jack Casement had said, but because it was evident that neither Katherine Casement nor Reed Owen had given Jack Casement all the facts. They'd left out just enough to put the onus of the affair on him.

That, he told himself fiercely, was to be expected of Reed Owen. But not from Kate Casement; he'd thought she was fairer than that. There was only one conclusion to make, and that was that she deliberately covered up for Owen, at his expense.

He shook himself. What the hell did he expect? She and Reed Owen were old friends, probably with a much deeper sentiment between them than mere friendship. While he . . . well, he was just a man who had ridden in out of the desert. . . .

He went on over to the wagon park and from the black shadow of a towering freighter Bill Yerkes's voice reached out at him. "All quiet, lad."

Roswell went over there, hunkered down against a high wheel, loaded his pipe. Here the night was still, but over to the west the voice of the town was a solid rumble, broken now and then by a high, wild yell as some exuberant spirit let loose an excess of energy.

"Be glad to get shut of this place," growled Yerkes. "When a man's been used to the quiet camps of the desert, all this racket and rush gets on his nerves."

Roswell did not answer and the grizzled teamster peered at him shrewdly in the dark. "The old man spur you some for that ruckus over at the warehouse this afternoon?"

Roswell was silent again, then finally answered. "Some. He hadn't had all the story."

"Hah," murmured Yerkes. He considered this for a moment, then added: "Now that I'd more or less expect from Reed Owen, but not of the girl."

Roswell changed the subject. "You wouldn't let me stand a guard shift, yet you take one yourself."

Bill Yerkes grunted cheerfully. "I'm a night hawk by preference. I like to sit and watch the stars. Brad Lincoln will be out to spell me at midnight."

Clay Roswell found himself drawing deep comfort from his pipe and this area of quiet. It was, he realized, the first time he had fully relaxed since signing on with Casement. The drive to get the wagons ready had lived with him night and day. Now it was done and, though no man could foresee the inevitable difficulties that lay ahead, for this moment at least he could settle back with the satisfaction of knowing he'd done, and done well, what Casement expected of him.

A quick-stepping figure was just an indistinct shadow, moving about among the wagons. "Casement himself," murmured Bill Yerkes. Then he raised his voice. "Over here, Mister Casement, if you're lookin' for somebody."

"Who is it?" asked Casement.

"Bill Yerkes and the lad, Clay Roswell."

Casement came over to them and spoke with a dry humor. "These wagons look pretty heavy and solid. I imagine they'll still be here at dawn."

"Aye," said Yerkes. "But Clay here, and myself, we decided it wouldn't hurt to play safe."

Casement dropped on his heels, dug a Virginia cheroot from a pocket, and lighted up. Bill Yerkes got to his feet. "Think I'll prowl a circle. A man can't see everything from here."

As Yerkes moved off into the night, Jack Casement said softly: "Good man, that."

"I'd never have been able to get things organized this quick if it hadn't been for Bill Yerkes," said Roswell. "If there's any credit due, most of it should go to him."

"Takes a good man to pick a good man," said Casement. He cleared his throat, spat. "Wasn't censuring you, over at the cabin, Clay. You've done a fine job and I appreciate it. I . . . didn't know that Reed Owen had laid hands on one of your men. You were quite right in not standing for that."

Some of the bleakness ran out of Roswell. This man was very fair. "Skip Keswick had to be backed up, sir. It was the only right thing to do. I'm sorry it had to happen, and I'm sure there'll be no more trouble of the sort."

Casement was silent for a moment. "Reed Owen has a streak of black temper in him, but he's a mighty good man for all that. He's done a tremendous job for me on the supply end."

Roswell kept his silence, so presently Casement went on, speaking another thought. "You got any idea of what lies ahead, Clay?"

Roswell answered gravely. "Some, I think. Long miles, rough country. Thirst, hunger, killing work. Indian trouble. Probably some dead men."

"All of that," Casement agreed. "And in years to come, some potbellied merchant will fume and curse over some slightly delayed message through the wire we string, with never a thought of the men who did the job."

Casement got to his feet, stretched. "Got to get over to the office. Promised Kitts I'd meet her there. Still some paperwork to clear up. You better go get some sleep. Long day ahead."

Roswell watched Casement disappear among the wagons. *Yeah,* he thought, a little savagely, *Kitts, with her blue eyes and shining, coppery head. Kitts, who hadn't told all the story of his argument with Reed Owen.* It was almost as though she had lied. And that wasn't a good thought.

He smoked out his pipe, tapped it against his boot heel, got up, and headed for one of the big general bunkhouses where the teamsters slept. When he turned in, he was completely weary, but able to sleep only fitfully. The tension of this thing had come back. He was up again in the final black hour before dawn, to breakfast at an eating house that catered to the teamsters who were late into this town, or early out of it.

At the wagon yard, things were electric with a mighty stir.

Sleepy, growling voices in the dark, the clank of harness and trace, the stamp and shuffle of mule teams being led into place. Dust, invisible in the dark, rose to bite the nostrils, lay an acrid bitterness across the tongue. Morning's chill was in the air. In the eastern heavens a grayness began to form and grow.

Clay Roswell, working a way through the dark tangle, heard a teamster swear in harsh surprise, then call a warning to one of his fellows.

"What the devil! Hey, Pike, careful with those mules. There's a damn' drunk layin' here, dead to the world. Nearly led my team right over him."

"Shake him awake and get him out of there," came the answer. "Somebody will run over him, sure, once we start to roll. Wait, I'll give you a hand."

There was a moment of grunting effort. Then: "Don't smell any likker on him. And he ain't limp . . . he's stiff. Hey, this man ain't drunk . . . he's dead!"

Gusty consternation broke. "Hey, Roswell, Clay Roswell! Bill Yerkes! Pass the word for Roswell or Yerkes. Trouble over here!"

Roswell hurried to the spot and a moment later Bill Yerkes came panting up. "What's this . . . what's this? What kind of trouble?"

"Found this feller layin' here. Thought first he was drunk. But by the feel of him, he's dead. Scratch a light, somebody?"

A sulphur match flared, its brief, small gleam throwing into harsh outline grim and wondering faces. It showed more. It showed a husky young teamster sprawled there, his hair matted with blood and dust.

"Brad Lincoln!" exclaimed Bill Yerkes harshly. "He's been clubbed to death!"

Before further words could be spoken, another yell lifted, up at the head of the line. "Who moved my wagon? Where's my wagon?"

"Now there could be an answer to this dirty business," growled Yerkes. "Come on, Clay."

They found Skip Keswick stamping around and swearing in a vast bewilderment.

"What kind of crazy business is this?" the little teamster was demanding of the world. "I left my wagon lined up right here. Now, it's gone!"

CHAPTER SIX

They left Fort Churchill in the dawn's shadowy grayness, men and wagons, like a small army advancing to do battle with the far-running wilderness of the desert's stubborn sage and with the aloof and hostile mountains that lay beyond. When the sun burst up across the world, it was looking them fairly in the eye with a blazing challenge, as though to remind them that here was another implacable enemy that would fight them down across the miles without mercy or let-up.

Out in the lead rolled the pole wagons, dropping off one of those tall and tapered timbers at regularly staked intervals. From twenty-five to thirty of these would be needed for every mile, depending on the type of terrain to be covered. As fast as a pole wagon was emptied, it would return to the yards at Fort Churchill for another load.

Other wagons put down crews to dig holes, set up and true the poles. Hard on the heels of these men came the wire-stringing crew and behind them all the vast welter of paraphernalia necessary to build and maintain and keep life in this thing after it was completed.

Cook wagons and wagons loaded with food and wagons loaded with water. Wagons hauling coils of wire and insulators and tools. Wagons loaded with batteries and carboys of acid and crated instruments. Wagons piled high with blanket rolls and camp gear for the crews, with fodder for the sweating, laboring mules and horses. Wagons loaded with sawed lumber and other building material necessary to construct relay and supply stations every thirty-five to fifty miles.

Sitting the saddle on a rangy buckskin horse, Clay Roswell watched this thing take form and movement in the first dawn, and knew a small and marveling moment over his part in it. How fast and far could a man's fortunes change? Such a very little time ago he was a penniless and jobless drifter, heading west mainly because it was a young land, calling to youth, and because that way lay the dim opportunity of slaking a stored-up and bitter thirst for vengeance.

Now he was part of this, and all these wagons and what they carried and how far and how well they rolled was his responsibility. And on how well he carried off that responsibility, the success of the great, brave undertaking would depend. This was a humbling thought.

Also humbling, was the memory of what the morning's start had disclosed. A good man—dead. Clubbed to death. A wagonload of flour gone. His responsibility there, too. The thought put a settled harshness across his face, as he rode ahead, watching what had been only a plan before, now become reality.

He watched the first poles dropped and set and he saw this job as a giant of enterprise, beginning a march toward a fated destiny. And each time a pole was set it meant another stride that the giant had taken, while all the winnowing dust clouds were the banners of brave advance.

A big spring wagon, with bows and canvas top, drawn by a team of four horses, came up at a trot. Driving it was Jack Casement, and riding the seat beside him was his daughter, her look one of grave stillness. Casement pulled in and set his brake, his face grim.

"That was a dirty business back at the yards, Clay. Sort of puts a cloud over the start of the job. Got any ideas?"

Clay shook his head. "Not yet. I left Bill Yerkes back there, to see if he can pick up any trace of the missing wagon. He'll be out to report after a while. If he hasn't found anything, I'm going to take a look myself. I feel responsible."

Casement swung his hand in a hard wave. "Hell, lad, not your fault. You were long-headed enough to put out a guard. You couldn't have done any more than that. It's just one of those things we'll have to write off. It won't be our last loss of either men or supplies. You can't cover a trail like we got up ahead, without paying a price. Well, I'll see you later in the day, up ahead."

In the brief moment it took for Casement to kick off the brake and get his outfit rolling again, the girl beside him flashed a direct look at Clay Roswell and he returned it with a cool inscrutability that made her flush, and, as the wagon rolled on, she was biting her lip.

An hour later, Bill Yerkes came up on a pole wagon, reporting no luck. "With a thousand sets of wagon tracks around Churchill, leadin' every which way, and with more cuttin' in all the time, tryin' to work out one set just can't be done, Clay."

"Maybe." Clay nodded. "But I'm going to have a try, just the same. You keep an eye on things up here, Bill. Especially the pole wagons. Keep them rolling!"

"Where you aim to look, boy?"

"Anywhere and everywhere. That wagon didn't grow wings and fly, Bill. Now Brad Lincoln went on guard at midnight. The town doesn't begin to quiet down until a couple of hours later. So it's a good guess that Lincoln was killed and the wagon taken somewhere around three or four in the morning. Which doesn't leave the thieves too much time to move and hide that wagon. It can't be too far away. So I'm going to have my look for it."

Clay rode straight back to town, to the scene of the jump-off at the wagon yard. Here he sat his saddle for a time, trying to picture this thing. Bill Yerkes had been quite right about wagon tracks. They led everywhere; the earth was a tangled maze of them. A man could do nothing there; he had to look above and past them. Which way the thieves?

Certainly not east into the desert, for that would have placed them directly in front of the massed advance of the other wagons and sure discovery. North would have taken them squarely up against the military reservation and the barrier that offered. Skip Keswick's wagon had been in the front rank to the east, so to have headed due west with it the thieves would have had to make a way through all the other massed wagons and then hit the very heart of town, with strong risk of discovery. So, Clay decided, south would be the only logical route, south and then perhaps a swing to the west, beyond the spread of the Pony Express corrals and freight headquarters. He swung his horse. He would try that way.

South of town he struck the Carson River and the emigrant route that followed its swing to the west. Although a full decade had passed since the initial great surge of emigrant trains had started west to the golden placers of California, Conestoga wagons were still rolling out the long miles and there were several camps along the river.

At some of these Clay stopped, looked things over, and asked blunt questions. Most of the camps met him fairly, but knew nothing that was of help to him. In one camp, however, he found surliness in a lank, bitter man.

"I ain't stole no wagonload of flour," growled the fellow. "But I'd sure steal me a couple of barrels of it, should I get the chance. And I'd feel no way bad about it. At least I'd be an honest thief. It's these traders and shopkeepers who are the real thieves at the prices they ask. An' they smirk an' play up as honest while they take a poor man's last dollar for the grub he needs to feed hisself and his family."

"It's a tough trail, friend," Clay told him laconically. "And no man can expect a free ride over it."

In time the river threw itself into a wide half loop and the road cut its way from point to point of this. Inside the loop was a thick growth of sour willow and alder. And it was here that Clay finally struck a lead. For wagon tracks swung off the road here and led into the willows, one set of broad tired tracks, several sets of smaller ones.

In themselves, these tracks did not necessarily mean anything, for they could lead to nothing more than another emigrant camp along the river. But just now no smoke of campfire winnowed above the willow and alder thickets and no sign of life showed anywhere.

Clay rode into the loop quietly, alert and tall in his saddle. In the boot under his knee was slung a Henry rifle, but it was the Dragoon Colt gun at his hip that he swung to a handier position. The wagon tracks led far into the loop, then broke abruptly into a small clearing. Clay reined up.

There, right in front of him, stood the missing wagon. It had not been damaged in any way that he could see, but it was empty. On the ground behind it was a single smashed barrel of flour, its powdered whiteness sifted out and badly trampled. Other sign was easy to read. The load from the big freighter had been transferred to several smaller and lighter wagons, which had been returned to the road and gone their several ways. It would be, Clay realized, useless to try and follow any farther. The fugitive wagons might be anywhere, scattered like a covey of quail.

He sat his saddle for some little time, reconstructing this thing. There were certain angles about it that no sane man could overlook. His face was grim as he went back to the road, heading east again. He pulled in at the camp of the surly emigrant.

"Found what I was looking for," he told the fellow laconically. "The wagon, I mean. The flour is gone, all except one barrel that was dropped and smashed. Most of what it held is pretty messy, but I think you might salvage fifteen or twenty pounds. You're welcome to it if you want it." Clay described the place where the wagon was hidden, turned to ride on, then paused, struck with another thought. "Where was it that you ran into those high prices, friend?"

The emigrant, friendlier now at promise of a few pounds of fresh flour, showed a mellowing attitude. "One place was Myers Wells, back out in the desert. Know what that damn' pirate wanted? Two dollars a pound! Yes, sir, two dollars a pound. How in God's name can a poor man pay that? Though some folks do, I reckon. Case of pay or have their wife and kids go hungry. Obliged for the flour. If it's usable at all, it means a heap to me."

Clay stopped at another camp farther along, one close to the road, questioning again a big, gaunt, bearded fellow. "I can't recall any special wagon goin' by last night," said the man. "Wagons of one kind or another are always movin' along this trace. You get so used to them you just don't pay 'em no attention one way or another. This one would have passed sometime before dawn this mornin', you say? Well, about that time I reckon I was sleepin' pretty sound. Sorry."

Clay made no further stops, but headed right on back out to the desert, where the tall poles were beginning their march to the east and where the first wire was already stretched in gleaming swoops. He located Bill Yerkes and told him where the wagon was.

"So that's how they did it, eh?" said Bill slowly. "Well, at least we get our wagon back, which we can sure enough use. I'll get along in, put together a hitch of mules, and go after it."

Now that this thing had begun, there was no let-up. The various crews shook down into their stride and a certain rhythm took over. Pole wagons coming and going beat up a never-clearing banner of dust. As quickly as a pole was set up and tamped and trued, there would be a man with climbing irons going up it and presently another graceful sweep of wire would be singing in the wind. Watching this thing take on concrete form and purpose, Clay could understand how truly Alex Majors had spoken when he said the days of the Pony Express were numbered.

Not all the going, of course, would be as swift and easy as these first few miles of desert. The toughest miles by far lay out ahead, and there would be plenty of them. There would be enormous dangers and difficulties to overcome, but in the end this thing would be done. That certainty was in the way all men worked and talked.

Skip Keswick, lacking a wagon of his own, had been given the outfit Brad Lincoln would have driven, a wagon loaded with wire and insulators. Spying the little teamster, Clay rode up beside him and told him of locating the stolen wagon.

"Now that's good news," Skip agreed. "But handlin' this outfit and rememberin' who should be up here on this box sure keeps me in a boil, boss. Brad Lincoln was a damn' good man. And every time I think of him bein' beat down and killed like he was. . . ." Skip shook a dour head, then burst out bitterly: "The damn' scurvy, murdering scum!"

"Rough, all right, Skip," agreed Clay. Then he added, a trifle grimly: "But Brad Lincoln won't be the only dead man this job will leave along the back trail."

Skip Keswick nodded. "That I can see, all right. When we hit the mountains and the rough goin' there, well, there'll be wagon accidents, outfits turnin' over, things like that. Then, fellers like him . . ."—Skip paused to nod toward one of the wire crew, working at the top of a pole—"they can't go skitterin' up and down them poles forever without somebody makin' a mistake and takin' a fall. Besides which, wait'll we get well into the Goshiute and White Knife country. Them Injuns will make things plenty warm. Yeah, we'll lose men. And while a dead man is a dead man, there's still a difference. There's such a thing as bein' killed legitimate on a job. But it's somethin' else when some thievin' whelp crawls up on you in the night and clubs your head in. Dyin' that way seems so . . . so damned useless."

When sundown marked the end of the day's effort, Clay rode slowly through the camp set up beside the route. Cooking fires gleamed ruddily in the twilight and about them the crews gathered and ate, then sought their blanket rolls to lounge and smoke and talk over what that day had held and what other days to come would hold. The atmosphere was one of contented weariness, but also of eagerness for the morrow. Which was, thought Clay, the way of men. Nothing pleased these men more than to build, and the more challenging the job, the greater its lure. Then there was the satisfaction of being part of something that would be marked and preserved in written history. Ten thousand telegraph lines might be built in the future, but this one carried a significance all its own.

Clay found Bill Yerkes at one of the fires and ate supper with him. Afterward they moved off a little to one side and had a smoke together.

"I looked over the sign around that wagon, Clay," said Yerkes thoughtfully. "Wonder did it suggest to you what it did to me?"

"Maybe," Clay said. "What's your idea, Bill?"

"That thing was planned careful and well in advance," said the teamster. "Everything points to that. They knew the exact wagon they wanted and they had the smaller wagons all set and ready to transfer the load. They had the exact spot picked where they'd hide out while they made the transfer. They had poor Brad Lincoln located and knew what they intended to do to him. No one man did the thievin', or no two men. It was a gang, organized and ready and figurin' everything sharp. How's that?"

"Go on." Clay nodded. "We agree, so far."

"Just as an instance, you take a ton of flour," said Yerkes. "You get it for nothin' by stealin' it. Then you sell it somewhere, for say a dollar a pound . . . and some of the tradin' posts along the fringe of things out here are askin', and gettin', more than that from some of the emigrant outfits who got to have it . . . and what have you got? Well, with a ton you got a couple of thousand dollars. And there was way better than a ton on Skip Keswick's wagon. Pretty good money for a night's work, Clay."

"We still agree, Bill," said Clay. "It's a trail that could go a long way and uncover many things. At the first chance I get I'm going to have a try at running that trail down. But in the meantime, let's keep our ideas to ourselves."

"Now that's all right with me," agreed Yerkes. "Lots of times if a man acts stupid enough, he can fool them who think they're smart. Right now you're rememberin' something that I remember, ain't you, boy?"

"It's a hell of a thing to think," said Clay. "But I'm remembering it." He stood up. "Now I'll go see what Jack Casement thinks of the first day's progress."

Clay had to ride well up ahead of the sprawling general camp before he located the canvas-topped spring wagon that was Jack Casement's traveling headquarters. There was a small fire burning beside it and on a tarp spread beside the flames Katherine Casement was busy laying out some supper utensils. She straightened as Clay Roswell moved into the firelight glow, and brushed a lock of hair back from her face. She made a slim and girlish figure and the fire's warmth had built a flush in her cheeks. Clay's expression was taciturn, unrevealing.

"Your father handy?" he asked quietly.

"He's over with Tom Hughes of the survey gang. He should be back for his supper at any time."

"Mind if I wait?"

"Why not? This is Dad's headquarters. All of the gang bosses report to him here."

Clay dropped down on his heels, got out his pipe again. Over the curling smoke of it, he stared into the fire.

Going on with her supper preparations, the girl stole guarded glances at him. He seemed as remote as the stars, virtually ignoring her presence, and annoyed anger deepened the flush in her cheeks. Abruptly her eyes flashed and her head went up.

"I know what you're thinking . . . and you're wrong."

Clay looked at her. "Yeah? What am I thinking?"

"You're thinking that in reporting that argument between you and Reed Owen at the warehouse, I didn't tell all of it to Dad."

"Well, you didn't, did you?"

"No . . . but not for the reason you think. I wouldn't be that small. I can't stand unfairness any more than I can pig-headedness."

Their glances locked and the girl's eyes were very steady. Clay tipped his head slightly. "Reckon I owe you an apology. You had your good reasons, I guess . . . though I don't know what they were."

"I'll tell you what they were," she said spiritedly. "I know what the success of this job means to Dad. His whole reputation . . . and it is a mighty fine one . . . is staked on it. For a year he's been planning and working and organizing it. He can't do it all alone. He's got to trust many other men. And he can't have any of his men carrying on a private feud of their own at the expense of the job. Such a thing is hurtful in the middle of the job. It was better all around that an understanding be had before the jump-off. That's why I told him about you and Reed

Owen, so he could bring you together and clear the air before the start."

Clay's pipe had gone out. He freshened it before answering. "Now all that makes sense, and I agree with it. But why didn't you tell your father about Owen slugging Skip Keswick?"

"Because it was over and done with and was something that wouldn't happen again. Reed was sorry for it. He told me he was. And telling Dad about it would only have made him angrier with Reed, and that wouldn't have accomplished anything, either. I . . . I. . . ." She fumbled to a stop.

"Forget it," said Clay gently. "Your motives were sound. I'm glad you told me."

Back in the dark, voices sounded, and the clump of hoofs. Jack Casement came striding in and with him was Reed Owen, leading a saddled horse. Owen's whole attention was for Katherine Casement. "Had to ride out and see how things were going, Kitts," he said. "Now if I'm in time for supper . . . ?"

She smiled and nodded. "You've a genius for showing up at eating time, Reed."

Reed Owen chuckled. "That's your fault. You're too good a cook."

Clay Roswell turned to Jack Casement. "Wanted to tell you that I found the wagon. But the flour was gone." He sketched in brief details.

Casement nodded. "Chunk of money in that flour to write off. But you can't write off the life of a good man. That hurts. Yet . . ."—he shrugged—"projects like this one always cost lives. Glad we have the wagon back. We'll need it. Outside of that, how's everything?"

"Very good, I'd say, sir. Things are shaking down and everybody seems to know what his job is. The spirit of the men is fine. They seem to be eager for tomorrow."

"Now that's what I want!" ejaculated Casement with satisfaction. "With spirit you can do anything. Keep those wagons rolling, lad."

Clay backed out of the light, got his horse. Casement was already sitting beside the tarpaulin, beginning to eat. But it was plain that this man's mind was not on food. It was reaching out ahead, to the miles and the mountains, to the drive and the toil and the danger yet to come. The job had Jack Casement by the throat now, and, if he'd been a trifle curt with Clay, he had not meant to be.

Clay understood that and felt no resentment. The little talk he had with Katherine Casement had helped a lot. The mere fact that she had wanted to explain matters to him proved that she was not entirely impervious to his presence. Yet, as he glanced again at the three of them, Katherine, her father, and Reed Owen, gathered about that cheery little fire, he had to realize that he was still an outsider, that there was something that held these three together that he owned no part of, and the thought shot a thread of loneliness through him. His final look was at Reed Owen, and somberness darkened his eyes.

CHAPTER SEVEN

Gray dawn again, and the stir of men with their might. Marching poles, singing wires. Long days, short nights, sweat, toil, and more sweat. Wagons rolling, mules straining and sneezing in the dust. Fort Churchill shrinking in the distance, then finally lost in the haze. Here was all the desert's lonely wilderness.

A week went by and then another and another, and now they began moving out of the sage desert and into the rising country that piled up finally into gaunt and sullen mountains. Here the digging crews began battling stubborn rock with their clanging tools. Gleaming wire swooped upward, toward the far heights. And finally there was a rock-ribbed pass and water seeping from the earth. Cedar Pass Springs. Here they built the first relay station.

Long as they might have been to others, to Clay Roswell the days were all too short. As the distance between Fort Churchill and the point of wire increased, the task of the wagons increased. Particularly the pole wagons. Miles of wire could be moved up by one wagon, but one wagon could only carry enough poles for a few hundred yards. And so they rolled, back and forth, long days for each round trip now along the dusty trail, instead of short hours. On the move long before daylight, still going long after dark. Dust, distance, the gray desert, and the hostile mountains.

Clay Roswell and his buckskin horse traveled this same trail, back and forth, up and down, checking wagons and loads and toiling teams. Checking men, too, and their reaction to the driving toil. Inevitably there were breakdowns. Inevitably shortened tempers brought on arguments and fights. Hidden flaws in men and equipment cropped up under the never-ending pressure and punishment. And all of these it was Clay's responsibility to repair and correct and arbitrate. The wagons had to keep rolling.

For days at a time Clay saw nothing of Jack Casement, for Casement was always far up ahead, throwing his tremendous energy into the keen and reaching edge of this thing, working with his survey gang and opening the trail. Locating stands of timber on the eastern swoop of the mountains and moving in pole-cutting crews to fell and trim and peel timbers to build up a fresh supply of poles, now that the yards at Fort Churchill were growing killingly distant and nearly empty, too.

From time to time Reed Owen showed, riding out from Fort Churchill, giving the word that he was checking up on the supply situation. conferring with Jack Casement, and, as Clay Roswell noted with no great pleasure, managing to spend considerable time in the company of Katherine Casement.

A day came when Casement sent word back along the line for Clay Roswell to report to him and that evening Clay caught up with the headquarters wagon. Casement greeted him heartily and told him to sit down to supper. Reed Owen was there beside the fire, talking with Katherine Casement and, though he greeted Clay casually, not far below the surface of his apparent affability lay the same old dislike and hostility. Katherine Casement replied to Clay's greeting gravely, neither unfriendly nor otherwise.

She was slim and brown and capable, and Clay thought, watching her, that here was one of those rare women who bloomed instead of withered under harsh sunlight and the comparative hardships of a rough and frugal trail. When she met Clay's eyes and recognized the admiration there, she colored faintly and grew increasingly busy about the fire.

Jack Casement was all a-boil with enthusiasm over the progress that had been made and the way the work was going. This man was a born builder, with a streak of the adventurer and explorer thrown in. He had every aspect of the job at his fingertips and bubbled with eager talk. There seemed no limit to the furious energy that surged in him.

"Things are moving better than I dreamed they could, Clay," he enthused. "We're well ahead of schedule and I got good news for you. Good news for you and your pole wagons. In a few days you'll be able to start hauling from the new pole yard on Frosty Creek."

"That I'm mighty glad to hear, Mister Casement," said Clay. "For the trail back to Fort Churchill is getting mighty long."

Casement dropped a hand on Clay's arm. "And I want you to know you've been doing a fine job, lad. And working like the very devil, haven't you?"

Clay bore visible proof of this. He was brown as an Indian, and leaned down to whipcord and rawhide. His eyes were deep-set, his face a trifle craggy. He showed a small smile. "I'm not complaining, sir. Work was what I asked for. I'm lucky, riding a smooth saddle. It's the men who pound out the miles on the wagons that my hat is off to. But the spirit of this thing has got them and they wouldn't trade places with a king."

Then, glancing at Katherine Casement, Clay spoke of something else that was on his mind. "The men have been picking up some talk back at Churchill. The Pony Express reports increasing Indian activity in the country we're now moving into. White Knives and Goshiutes, mainly. I hope you'll remember that, Mister Casement, when this wagon of yours is working way out ahead."

Reed Owen spoke with open scoffing. "Some jarhead is

always starting Indian scare talk. I've been in Fort Churchill for the large part of a year now, and I haven't seen hide nor hair of an Indian except a few rag-tag Shoshones. And they're about as dangerous as scary and whipped dogs."

"The kind of Indians I'm telling about you don't see in Fort Churchill . . . or even close to it," stated Clay dryly. "Wide difference between the Shoshones and the Goshiutes, and this is Goshiute country."

Owen glanced at the Dragoon Colt gun swinging at Clay's lean middle. "How many of these ferocious savages have you used that popgun on, Roswell?"

"None . . . yet," said Clay quietly. "And I hope I never have to. But any man's a fool to ignore a danger that every experienced desert man knows to be real."

Reed Owen flushed angrily at the tartness of Clay's words and tone and would have blurted an angry answer if Jack Casement hadn't spoken first.

"Clay's right, Reed. Next general supply wagon coming out, I want you to send along those crates of Henry rifles and ammunition we got back in the warehouse. This is what they were purchased for. Clay, put one of those rifles on every wagon and I'll see that there are a couple handy to every one of the gangs. Also, I'll keep a couple on this wagon. A gun is something you may never need, but if you do, there's nothing to take its place. And now, Reed, let's you and me go over and see Tom Hughes of the survey gang. There's a certain kind of scale paper he wants sent out and he can give you a better idea of what it is than I can."

Reed Owen went off into the night with Casement, showing a certain reluctance, and Clay, noting this, smiled faintly as he looked across the fire at Katherine Casement.

"Friend Owen acts like he's afraid I might grab you up and fly off with you the minute his back is turned."

She showed that old challenging toss of her coppery head. "Reed knows better than that. He knows I'd have plenty to say about it, myself."

"Yeah," admitted Clay, "you probably would. But I've got to admit the temptation is there. Now a campfire is nearly always a pretty thing, and not every woman can work around one and still be the heart of the picture."

She looked at him, faint color stirring in her cheeks. "What wearies me most are glib and empty compliments, Mister Clay Roswell."

"Suppose they're not meant to be empty or glib? Can you give me any good reason why I shouldn't admire you? And say so with all respect? And haven't we known each other long enough now to drop the formality . . . Kitts?"

The color in her cheeks deepened. "I believe I'm the one to decide on that."

"Of course. And I'm asking you to."

She turned partially away from him, began gathering up the supper dishes. "I see dozens of men every day. And you're just one of them."

The musing ease Clay had known, relaxed here beside this fire and in the presence of this girl, went swiftly away. His eyes pinched down and his face pulled into bleak lines. He got to his feet. His tone ran harsh.

"Yeah, that's me. Clay Roswell. Just another of the hired hands. Still, I don't know why you should toss a brickbat like that at me. I really don't know why, but you make it pretty definite, Miss Casement, so I promise you I won't bother you again. Tell your father I couldn't wait to get back on the job. I'm known there as Clay."

He stalked over to his horse and rode away. The girl stood, biting her lip. Then she went to work on the dishes again, shucking them together a little fiercely.

"Sometimes, Katherine Casement," she told herself hotly, "sometimes you have the meanest tongue in the world. What on earth's the matter with you? He meant nothing wrong."

CHAPTER EIGHT

A pole wagon, toiling up the rough climb into the mountains, broke a pole bar. Clay Roswell, Bill Yerkes, and the muleskinner of the outfit toiled in the baking heat and acrid dust, repairing the break. Reed Owen, on his way back to Fort Churchill, rode by. He said nothing, but he looked at Clay with surly eyes.

Bill Yerkes, scrubbing sweat and dust from his face, said: "There rides a jigger I just can't figger out, Clay. What's he got against you? Is he still nursin' his mad over the argument we had that day with him when he wanted to overload Skip Keswick's wagon?"

The muleskinner, reaching for the water bag slung to the side of his wagon, said: "Just plain ornery, that's Owen. Back at Churchill, without Casement around, he's always snappin' and snarlin' at the boys. Don't see how Jack Casement can stand him."

"He knows how to keep the supplies coming," observed Clay briefly. "The rest doesn't matter too much."

One day was pretty much like another. The pattern didn't vary and the days were all full of toil. Clay drove himself harder than ever, so that at night he could lose himself in the sleep of deep weariness instead of lying and watching the stars and thinking about a slim, coppery-haired girl who had faced him across a campfire and dismissed him with a remark that cut like a whiplash.

He had thought over that moment a hundred times since it

happened, and he still couldn't understand it. Unless she still held it against him for winning his point the day of his argument with her and Reed Owen at the warehouse. But that didn't make sense, either. She was too intelligent to hold a senseless grudge. Also, while there was no real reason why she had to, she had still seemed fairly anxious to square herself by explaining why she had not reported that incident more fully to her father. That one fact alone had made Clay feel that she was not entirely uninterested in him. Yet, the first time he had tried to open the door to a more relaxed and friendly basis, she had slammed it shut in his face in no uncertain fashion.

Well, he mused bleakly, even the dumbest man could get the idea, once he'd been kicked in the teeth solidly enough. By this time he should be smart enough to quit thinking about her—to forget her entirely. But he found that wanting to forget, and being able to, were birds of entirely different plumage. That was the pure hell of it.

At another day's sundown, another wagon rolled in, heavily loaded and tarp-covered. The muleskinner, after caring for his mules, came over to Bill Yerkes, carrying a whip. "Where's Danny Huggins, Bill?" he asked. "He up ahead somewhere?"

"No," answered Yerkes. "Not up ahead. Danny's back at Churchill, after a load of grub."

"Devil he is!" growled the muleskinner. "He left Churchill a good four hours ahead of me. I know, because I was talkin' with him just before he kicked off the brake. I was joshing him, telling him I'd probably catch up and pass him, even though he was gettin' a full half day start on me. You missed him, Bill. He must have gone through without you seein' him."

"Nobody goes through without me seeing them, Sash," Yerkes retorted. "I tell you, Danny ain't here. You must have passed him along the road somewhere and didn't know it. You must have been sleepin'."

"Sleeping, hell!" exploded Sash. "I don't sleep on the job. Besides, this is his whip. That's what I want to see him about. I found it layin' beside the road. Quit joshin' me, Bill. Where is he?"

Bill Yerkes stared at the muleskinner. This man was giving him a straight story. Bill said: "Come on, Sash. Clay Roswell will want to know about this."

Clay listened to the muleskinner's story, a shadowed look growing in his eyes. Of Bill Yerkes he asked: "You say Danny Huggins was to bring in a wagon of grub, Bill?"

"That's right. Flour and bacon."

Clay turned to Sash. "How do you know this is Danny's whip?"

"Because I watched him whittle out the handle from a piece of mountain ash, and saw him carve his name all fancy on the butt of it. See here?"

Clay examined the whip. "And just where did you find it, Sash?"

"Down where the road cuts through them little sand valleys just before tying into the start of the main climb. Clay, you don't think . . . ?"

"Sash, I don't know what to think. But I intend to find out. Did you notice anything else? Like tracks where a wagon might have turned off the road?"

Sash shook his head dejectedly. "No, I didn't. Hell, I never even gave anything like that a thought. I just happened to see the whip layin' there, shucked down after it, and climbed back up without even stoppin' my outfit, it bein' plenty slow goin' about there. Goddlemighty, you're not thinkin' that something might've happened to Danny? Injuns, mebbe . . . or . . . ?"

"I'm not saying anything right now, Sash," cut in Clay. "We're sure of just two things. Danny Huggins left Fort Churchill, but he didn't arrive here. The answer has to be back along the road somewhere. I'm going looking for it. Bill, you're in complete charge until I get back."

"You think maybe Casement should know about this?" Yerkes hesitated. "A thing of this sort should be his worry, not yours, Clay."

"He's got plenty of other things to worry about, Bill. And I'm responsible for the wagons and the men who drive them. Now you two keep this thing under your hats. For there's no need of getting the other men worked up."

Five minutes later Clay was sending his buckskin down the long sweep toward the distant desert.

It was long after dark when he reached the little sand valleys and only the stars to give off a faint, but insufficient glow. But Clay knew there would be a moon later, so he rested the buckskin and waited stoically. When the moon finally climbed into view and made of these tangled, twisted little valleys a land of spectral loneliness, Clay began to ride again.

He tried the south side of the road first, paralleling it, but found nothing to break the smooth, silvery sweep of the sand areas among the scattered sage clumps. So he cut across the north and took up the search there. And here, finally, plainly showing under the moon's growing brilliance, he found what he was looking for. A set of broad wagon tracks, breaking off the main road and winding up one of the little valleys, the sign plainly on sandy earth that had never before known the print of wagon tracks.

Clay followed the sign at a jog, his senses keen and alert. The little valley twisted back and forth, as though formed by the passage of some mammoth snake, but presently and abruptly it broke into a little, almost circular flat and here Clay reined in sharply, the buckskin sidling and snorting softly. Here a dark and crumpled bulk lay sprawled under the moon. A man. Danny Huggins. Quite dead. Shot through and through.

Clay straightened from examining the luckless teamster, swung back to the saddle, and headed on, speeding up the pace. These little valleys made a miniature badlands, an area about a mile wide and five miles long. Just inside the northern edge he found the wagon, with the string of mules still standing wearily in harness.

The wagon was empty and the betraying sign all around told the same story as that on the morning when Clay had tracked down Skip Keswick's stolen wagon. This wagon's load had been transferred to several smaller ones, and of course there was no sight of these, only of their tracks, leading north and west.

It took no deep reasoning to know where these wagons would lose their sign. North lay the main emigrant route, churned and worn and dusty. Marked and re-marked by all the other wagons that had passed and were still passing. No use to try and work out a trail there. This thing had to be gone at another way.

Smart, these murdering thieves were, mused Clay savagely. As before, they had figured everything out carefully—time, distance, necessary equipment, and location. They took foodstuffs that could not be identified, but they left wagon and mules that could. And a dead man who would never talk. Danny Huggins.

Clay tied the buckskin at lead behind the empty freighter, climbed to the box, got the mules into movement, and swung the outfit around and went back the way he had come. He stopped for the lonely and grisly chore of single-handedly getting a dead man into the wagon, and then went on to the main road, swinging into it, and heading west for the long, slow ride across the desert to Fort Churchill. He kept thinking about Danny Huggins back there on the bed of the wagon, making his final ride.

It was through the dawn's thin, steel-gray, chill light that Clay rolled the outfit up to the yards at Fort Churchill. Some teamsters, who had bedded for the night at the yards, were up and stirring, making ready for the start of another long haul out to point of wire. Clay turned the body of Danny Huggins over to them, listened to their cursing anger and dismay.

"This makes two of the boys," rapped one of them. "Brad Lincoln and Danny Huggins. What are you going to do about it, Roswell?"

"All I can," answered Clay grimly. "I got a couple of ideas I'm going to run down."

"Injun work, you think?" asked another.

"No. I got some respect for an honest Indian renegade. But for the white scum who pulled this . . . !" Clay swung a hand in a hard, cutting gesture. "You boys ride with your eyes open and a gun handy. You see anything suspicious along the trail, shoot first and ask questions later. For it seems it's become that kind of a trail."

Clay Roswell had some ideas, all right. He'd had them ever since the affair of Skip Keswick's wagon. He had not written off that incident, even through all the driving work. To the contrary, he'd thought of it many times. And he'd thought about this latest affair all during the long drag across the desert. Of one thing he was certain. No one man, or even a group of several men, could consume all the food that had been stolen. Behind these thefts was another purpose. It had to be that of selling the plunder somewhere. There had to be an outlet for this. He had to locate the outlet. Once he had that, he'd have something definite to go on and he could backtrack from there to the guilty parties.

He'd had a sleepless night, but he gave no thought to that, consumed as he was with the drive for action in this thing. He waited only long enough to buy and eat a breakfast, and then went out to the company's warehouse. There he accosted a yawning warehouse hand who told him that Reed Owen wasn't around, that he'd gone back up into the Sierras somewhere, to try and trace down some supplies that were considerably overdue from Sacramento.

"What you want to see him for?" ended the warehouse hand, grinning. "Another argument about an overloaded wagon?"

"No, something else," said Clay. "Maybe you can help me. Who do we get most of our flour from?"

"We get all of it from Abbott and Ives, of Sacramento," was the answer. "I know. I've checked off plenty of invoices. Flour from Abbott and Ives, bacon from Jansen and Son. I know it by heart."

"Got some in the warehouse?" asked Clay.

"Plenty!"

"Can I take a look at it?"

"Sure. Come on."

It was cavernous and gloomy inside the warehouse, and full of the mingled and pleasant odors that stored foodstuffs gave off. Barreled flour and cased bacon were stacked high.

"Plenty of money tied up in those piles," said the warehouse hand. "Take that flour, for instance. Costs us fifty dollars a barrel, laid down here. And we buy in big lots, as you can see. Some of the way stations along the main route across the desert and over the mountains ask as high as a hundred and fifty a barrel or even more . . . and get it, so I hear tell. Highway robbery, of course. But grub's the scarce item this side the mountains, so them who have it to sell, put on all the traffic will bear."

Clay examined one of the barrels closely. Stenciled across the top were the words: *Abbott & Ives, Sacramento*.

"Any other identifying marks?" Clay asked.

The warehouse hand shook his head. "Nothin' that Abbott and Ives put on outside their name. We mark each barrel as we check it off on the incoming load, like this." He pointed to a rough cross scrawled on the side of the barrel with a blue mark-ing crayon. "That's just so we'll know the barrel's been counted. Why you checking up? Shortages showing up somewhere?"

"You might call it something like that," admitted Clay dryly. "Now I wonder what kind of flour is being sold by these supply posts along the emigrant route?"

"Almost bound to be Abbott and Ives, or Valley Milling, I guess. Far as I know they're the only two outfits who supply flour in these parts. Valley Milling holds the contract with the Pony Express. They ship out of Sacramento, too."

Clay stood for a time in thoughtful silence, then nodded. "Obliged to you, friend. Everything running smoothly at this end of the job?"

"Couldn't be better. There's times when Reed Owen can be a mean son-of-a-bitch, but you got to give him credit. He sure knows how to handle supplies. And he's plenty shrewd . . . got a fine head for business. How are things going out at point of wire?"

"Moving," answered Clay succinctly. He showed a faint smile. "They've got to, with Jack Casement on the job. Well, once more . . . thanks for your trouble. Now I got to be pushing along."

CHAPTER NINE

Bear Wallow was a timber-rimmed flat up on the east slope of the Sierras. Here a busy little stream of cold, sweet water foamed out of a side gulch, spread into a series of pools across the flat, then ducked noisily into the timber below. There were several log buildings and a fair expanse of corrals. Here was a stage station serving the Concords that rocked and sped back and forth across the Sierras, and one of the buildings housed a supply post, trading with the emigrant families making the long trek into the sundown land beyond the mountains.

It was well along in the afternoon when Clay Roswell rode a weary buckskin horse into the flat. Clay carried a heavy load of fatigue on his own shoulders and the weight of it seemed to thin and harshen his face. He had himself a good look around, then dismounted stiffly, and went into the supply post. It was gloomy in here and the man who moved up out of the shadows was a heavy man, carrying a paunch, the weight of which seemed to narrow his shoulders and pull them into a slight stoop. His face was full of loose folds, and his eyes were hooded and beady on either side of a big, hungry nose. The man watched Clay, without speaking.

"Your place?" asked Clay, glancing around.

The man's voice had ruffles in it, like his sagging face. Also, it carried a certain truculence. "What d'you want?"

"How's the price of flour?"

"Hundred and fifty a barrel . . . take it or leave it."

"That's plenty steep," Clay said. "Lot cheaper than that back at Fort Churchill."

The fellow shrugged his sagging shoulders. "Go back there and get it, then. My price is my price. You damned jayhawkers make me sick and tired. You want grub . . . oh, yes! You want flour and you want hog belly. You're hungry, of course . . . and your women and your kids are hungry. You got to eat, you got to have grub. But you don't want to pay for it. You think it's a free world? You think I'm in business for my health?"

"Well, no," conceded Clay, falsely meek. "But a hundred and fifty dollars a barrel! Why, I can remember back home. . . ."

"You should have stayed home, maybe," cut in the paunchy one callously. "Go cry some place else." He started to turn away.

"Wait," said Clay. "I didn't say I wouldn't buy. Sure I was aiming to bargain. A man that don't bargain ain't smart. What brand of flour do you handle? Is it a good brand?"

"Abbott and Ives," was the grunted reply. "None better."

There were several barrels stacked at one end of the room. Clay moved over to them. The thin light that came in the open door fell obliquely across them. All carried the stencil *Abbott & Ives*. And on the side of one of them there had been some scraping done, either with a knife or some other sharp instrument, the scraped area showing up newer and brighter than the rest of the surface wood of the barrel. That lighter area shaped a rude cross.

"If you're goin' to buy," growled the paunchy one, "make up your mind. Either you want it or you don't. I tell you I'm sick of hagglin', whinin' trail tramps."

Clay, his eyes pinching down and turning cold, ran a finger over the scraped area on the side of the barrel. "Looks like a mark of some kind had been scraped off here. Now I wonder if that mark could have been a cross in blue? Hold it! I said hold it! Stay put . . . right there!"

The gun at Clay's hip came away, settled into line. For the paunchy one, a sudden wariness beginning to glitter in his little, hooded eyes, had started to sidle toward the rough counter at the rear of the room. Now the menace of Clay's gun stopped him in his tracks and he burst out with rough bluster.

"What is this . . . a hold-up?"

"Not exactly," shot back Clay. "But I want a little information. Where did you get that flour?"

"My business."

"And mine, too. Where'd you get it?"

"Still my business. You better put that gun away and get out of here while you're still able to. Plenty of people at this flat besides us. And I'm well thought of here. You start trouble and you'll be lucky if you're able to leave on your hands and knees."

There was more to this paunchy, ponderous man besides bulk. There was meanness in him and crookedness. But there was also nerve of a sort.

Clay Roswell had come a long way on the trail of this stolen flour. With him had ridden the memory of Brad Lincoln, dead of a clubbed-in head. And of Danny Huggins, dead of a treacherous bullet. Beyond that lay the picture of good men and true, toiling across the desert and the bleak forlorn mountains, pitting their strength and purpose against a hostile wilderness as they built for a better world. Men who had the right to go on with their task without being preyed on by such as this.

The chill in Clay's eyes deepened and he prowled down on the paunchy one. "If I leave here on my hands and knees," he said bleakly, "you won't be around to see me go. You'll be dead as hell. Maybe you think I'm backing a bluff. Well. . . ."

Clay reached and slapped, the heavy bulk of the gun tipping his swinging arm. The paunchy one tried to jerk his head aside, but didn't get it far enough. The barrel of the gun caught him, angling across his mouth and one pouchy cheek. The sodden impact wasn't enough to knock him completely off his feet, for Clay hadn't intended it to. But it did drop the fellow to his knees, and he hunkered there, like some great, misshapen ape, blinking dazedly, heavy lips sagging and blood fanning down across his chin.

"That," gritted Clay, "is just the start. You still think I'm bluffing? Mister, you're going to talk if I have to cut it out of you, word by word, with the barrel of this gun. Now, last chance. Who'd you buy that flour from . . . if you bought it?"

The paunchy one stared up at Clay, red murder in his beady eyes, and now he recognized fully the cold, implacable purpose of this lean, desert-burned man who stood over him. He saw that Clay Roswell meant every word he'd spoken. He rolled his tongue across his lips and spat crimson.

"All right," he mumbled thickly. "I bought it from two fellers named Pickard. Yeah, from Jess and Hoke Pickard. That's the truth of it."

Clay Roswell went very still for a moment, then ejaculated slow words. "The Pickards. Of course, the Pickards. Now that makes sense of everything."

It not only made sense, it brought a whole picture into focus that left Clay almost breathless with its broad implications. His gun sagged at his side and his head lifted as he stared at all the tangibles and intangibles of that picture. And it was at this unguarded moment that the paunchy one, driving forward from his knees, smashed the bulk of his rounded shoulders against Clay's legs, knocking him backward.

Clay landed on the broad of his back, his head banging wickedly on the rough puncheon floor, and for a moment he lay there, dazed. Then a pawing, cursing, frantic bulk crashed down on him. A clawing hand tried to tear the gun from Clay's fingers, a mauling fist beat at his face. Heavy knees dug at his midriff.

For a moment Clay took his punishment, unable to fight back. Then pain, surging through him, jerked him out of his daze. His fingers locked anew about a gun half wrenched from him. He rolled his head aside and caused another ponderous blow to miss him. He brought his left hand up, smashed the heel of it under a grinding, blood-slimed chin, snapped the arm straight, and drove the paunchy one's head up and back with a hard jerk.

This seemed to lift much of the smothering bulk off Clay and he twisted partially free. The paunchy one, feeling the advantage of his surprise attack slipping away from him, grabbed at Clay's rigid left wrist with both hands, jerking Clay's hand from under his jaw. This was a mistaken move, for it left Clay's gun hand free for the necessary second.

Clay slammed the bulk of the gun at the fellow's temple, but it didn't get high enough. It landed against the side of the neck, but it was enough to knock the paunchy one clear. Clay rolled over, came to one knee as the paunchy one, partially recovering, tried to lunge back at him. This time Clay was set for him and he clubbed with the gun again, getting plenty behind it. It crunched solidly home to the side of the paunchy one's head and he slumped down completely, in a senseless, bloody bulk.

Clay got to his feet, reeling a little unsteadily. In a few brief seconds he'd taken a wicked amount of punishment. There was blood on him, some of it the paunchy one's, some of it his own. His face was numb, his head ringing. Breath rasped hoarsely in and out of him; those heavy knees in the midriff had done him no good at all. He backed over to a wall, got his shoulders against it, and leaned there, feet spread, waiting for his breath to come fully back.

He shook his head, scrubbed a shirt sleeve across his eyes and face. Things began to steady down. His hat lay on the floor and he moved over and recovered this. He stood for a moment, looking down at the paunchy one, who still lay exactly as he'd gone down from the final belt from Clay's gun.

Clay's thoughts began to move more orderly again. One thing was sure—the quicker he got away from this place now, the better. If someone should happen in at the trading post, explanations might be awkward and difficult. Clay holstered his gun, gave his face another wipe with his shirt sleeve, headed for the door. And it was at this moment that a voice from outside called with harsh impatience.

"Hey, Bib . . . Bib Henry! Damn it man, are you deaf? Bib Henry, come out here!"

Plainly, by the tone of it, that voice had called before. But just as surely, Clay Roswell hadn't heard it until now. That brief, but savage struggle had blotted out all other sound and action.

Moving warily, Clay stopped just inside the door, using the deepening gloom of the place as cover, while he looked outside. The flat was all in shadow now. Tucked up here in the timber on the great eastern flank of the Sierras, the afternoon sun was long gone from this Bear Wallow Flat, and now a thickening and early twilight washed across the clearing like blue smoke.

Pulled up outside the trading post was a medium-sized, canvas-covered wagon, with two men on the seat of it. Now one of them began climbing down. For a moment the blue, smoky twilight made things a trifle vague to Clay's glance. Then recognition hit him like some tremendous blow.

That man just descended from the wagon was Jess Pickard, and the one still on the seat was Jess's brother, Hoke. The Pickards, both of them.

For a long moment Clay went still under the shock of recognition. Then a mixture of the old hate and the new purpose, based on what he'd learned from that senseless bulk lying on the floor behind him, sent Clay prowling through the door and out into the clear beyond. His challenge rapped flatly across the twilight calm.

"How'll I do instead of Bib Henry?"

For a thin and straining moment the Pickards stared like men who couldn't believe what their eyes told them stood before them. Then it was Jess Pickard, frantically going for a gun while Hoke, whirling, began grabbing at something behind the seat of the wagon.

CHAPTER TEN

It seemed to Clay Roswell that his muscles were almost maddeningly deliberate in answering the will of his thought. When he had clubbed down Bib Henry, action and thought had been as one. But now. . . . There was Jess Pickard, burly and half crouched, and there was a gun in the man's fist, stabbing level. The flame from it was a pale flicker in the twilight and the report of it was a flat echo that rocketed back and forth across the flat, trapped and held in the darkening timber all about. It was as though a faint, swift breath had touched Clay Roswell's cheek, and then a bullet, biting into the long wall behind him, made a small, splatting thud.

Jess Pickard, knowing he had missed that first shot, cursed and let go a second too hastily, and so missed again. Then Clay's gun was out and up and in line. The sight lost itself against Jess Pickard's burly chest. Then the recoil of the gun hammered back against Clay's wrist and the bounce of the weapon momentarily blotted out his target. He cocked the gun and brought it down into line again.

There was Jess Pickard, still on his feet. But Jess was crouched lower than before and was weaving a little from side to side, his bared and set teeth drawing a line across the dark shadow of his face. Jess shot a third time, but the slug hit way short, digging up a gout of sod not twenty feet in front of him. For Jess was toppling forward now and Clay's second bullet took him so and brought him over still faster, jackknifed at the waist. Jess struck on the side of his face and the point of his left shoulder in a spinning twist that turned him on his back. His heels drummed once as the life ran out of him. Then he was completely inert, seeming to shrink into the ground.

But Hoke—what about Hoke Pickard? Hoke had brought a rifle into sight from behind the wagon seat and was swinging the lever of the weapon as, half sitting, half standing, Hoke tried to get the muzzle in line with the man who had just killed his brother. Hoke might have been in time if he hadn't wasted the vital moment in glancing at Jess's sprawled bulk and yelling: "Jess! Jess!"

Clay Roswell used the same fine, but fast care on Hoke as he'd used on Jess. The Dragoon Colt slammed its flame and report a third time.

Knocked back across the seat of the wagon, Hoke Pickard writhed and flopped like a stepped-on snake and the rifle slid from his hands and clattered down across the off front wheel. Hoke, still writhing, grabbed at his right shoulder. Clay Roswell moved quickly in on him.

"I meant a better shot than that, Hoke. If I have to, I'll send the next one really deep. Don't make any play for that knife of yours!"

Hoke quieted a little, staring at Clay with numbed and venomous eyes. Clay gave a little wave with his weapon. "Come down off that wagon!"

Hoke came down, shaky and sliding, then stood holding to the wheel with his sound hand, steadying himself. He swung his head and laid another long look on Jess's shadowy figure, there against the patient earth. Then he sighed deeply and collapsed.

The challenge of those echoing shots had reached far and now several men broke into sight about the stage station and came warily across the flat. They stopped a few yards distant, staring.

"What goes on here?" demanded one of them. "What is this?"

"Part the settling of an old score, part the settling of a new one," answered Clay Roswell curtly. "A couple of thieves."

"Now that's your say-so, mister. But how do we know . . . ?"

"You don't," cut in Clay. "You'll have to take my say-so, which is good enough for me."

Now another man came hurrying up, a gaunt, long-jawed man with an air of authority about him. The others made way for him. He stared at the Pickards.

"Dead?" His voice ran harsh.

"One of them," said Clay. "The one by the wagon has a smashed shoulder from the way he acted."

The gaunt man looked Clay up and down. "You did the shooting?"

"Some of it. That one"—Clay pointed at Jess Pickard—"was trying for me. You can see his gun there. The one by the wagon was trying to get at me with that rifle."

"You know who they are?"

"I know. Jess and Hoke Pickard. A pair of damned thieves, and worse."

Another of the staring group spoke up. "I thought I heard somebody yellin' for Bib Henry, just before the shootin' started. Let's ask Bib. Mebbe he can tell us something about this. Where is Bib? You'd thought he'd've been out here by now, with all the ruckus going on."

"You'll find Bib Henry inside, either still out cold or nursing a bad headache. I had to get rough with him, too . . . gun-whipped him. You see, he's one of the gang, too. One of the gang of thieves." Clay watched them all warily as he spoke.

The gaunt man stared again at Jess and Hoke Pickard. Then he said: "I'm Jim Blaine, in charge of the stage station. I'm more or less responsible for everything that goes on in this flat." His glance lay searchingly on Clay Roswell. "There's a ring of truth in the way you talk, friend, but I'm taking it on myself to make damned sure about all of this. You and me are goin' to have a talk." He turned to one of the group. "Pike, you go see how Bib Henry is makin' it. Rest of you take a look at that feller yonder by the wagon. If he's just crippled up some, see what you can do for him."

"And don't let him get away," put in Clay. "He belongs to me."

Jim Blaine jerked his head and Clay followed him off to one side. The man who had gone into the trading post at Blaine's order stuck his head out the door.

"Bib's here, all right, like that feller said, with a beat-up head. Bib's beginnin' to shift around some, but he ain't goin' to be doin' any clear thinkin' for quite some time. What'll I do with him?"

"Throw some water on him," answered Blaine. He turned to Clay. "Let's have it?"

Clay had quieted now, the fever of what had taken place running out of him, leaving him feeling weary and subdued and queerly hollow inside. His voice ran quiet.

"You know Jack Casement?"

Blaine nodded. "Sure I know him. While he was settin' things up for that big job he's on now, he was back and forth across the mountains a lot of times. More'n once he stopped over at this station. Yeah, I know Jack Casement well."

"Casement is my boss," said Clay. "My name is Roswell. I'm Casement's wagon boss. Since we started on the big job, two of our supply wagons, both loaded with flour, have been robbed. Two of our teamsters have been murdered by the thieves. I've been trying to run down where that flour went to. I just found some of it in that trading post yonder."

"How do you know it's stolen flour?" demanded Blaine.

"Like this," explained Clay. "We buy all our flour from Abbott and Ives. You'll. . . ."

"That's nothing," broke in Blaine. "So do we."

Clay made a weary gesture. "Let me finish. When a shipment of flour comes in to our warehouse at Fort Churchill, each barrel has a tally mark put on it as it's checked in. A cross with blue marking crayon. You take a look at the flour in the trading post you'll see where that cross has been scraped off the barrels. It shows up plain. Now, I haven't seen the inside of that wagon yonder, but I wouldn't be surprised to find it loaded with flour, and, if it is, I'll bet that blue crayon cross is on every barrel, or the sign where it was scraped off will show up if you look careful enough."

"That," said Blaine, "is an idea. We'll look."

There was flour in the wagon, all right—ten barrels of it. A lantern had to be brought to furnish light enough to see, but it showed that every barrel bore a blue crayon check mark on it.

"Trying to scrape the mark off must have been Bib Henry's own idea," said Clay. "But I think I've proved my point."

"Yeah," agreed Blaine, the station agent, soberly. "You have. You figure Bib was one of the thieves?"

"That I couldn't say." Clay shrugged. "But he knew damned well that the flour he was handling was stolen. Which makes him just about as bad."

"What you aim to do with him?"

"That's up to you. You say you're responsible for how things are run on this flat. If you want a fellow like Henry around, that's your business. But the flour in the trading post belongs to Jack Casement's company, and we want it back. I'll drive this wagon and its load back to Churchill, myself. And I'll send a wagon out to pick up the rest. I'll be taking the crippled one, Hoke Pickard, back with me. Any objections to that plan?"

Jim Blaine shook his head gravely. "None at all. You've given me a straight story, Roswell, and the facts back you up. I'll see that the flour in the trading post is kept safe until your man calls for it. As for Bib Henry, I think I'll point him west and tell him to keep traveling. He always was a surly devil. I think this flat can get along without him."

An hour later, with the buckskin horse coming along on lead at the rear, Clay Roswell was driving a canvas-covered wagon loaded with ten one hundred pound barrels of flour down the blackness of the mountain road. On a pad of blankets just behind the seat, Hoke Pickard, bandaged and sick and venomously hating, also made the ride, which was turning out to be a long one for Clay.

He'd had a sketchy meal, back at Bear Wallow Flat, but now it was weariness—one dragging, bone-deep ache within him—that he had to fight. He tried to remember when he'd slept last and that time seemed incredibly far off. And he couldn't afford to sleep now. He had to get Hoke Pickard back to Fort Churchill, and then go farther along this trail he'd worked out. So he set his jaw, fought off the weariness, and stoically rode the long miles through.

CHAPTER ELEVEN

One of the long bunkhouses by the freight yards at Fort Churchill held a full dozen angry, grim-faced teamsters. One of these was Sash Perkins, who had found Danny Huggins's whip by the side of the trail, out where it ran through the little sand valleys. Sash was keeping a stern eye on Hoke Pickard who, pale and haggard, was huddled on one of the bunks. There was still venom in Hoke's eyes, but also there was a great fear.

For Hoke had heard these teamsters talking and the talk had been about a rope and a tree limb along the bank of the Carson River. Another thing that was wearing on Hoke was the knowledge that his brother Jess was dead. Not that he owed any special affection, as one brother to another, for Jess. But he'd always left the thinking up to Jess; however Jess figured a deal, that had been good enough for Hoke. Jess always had had an answer or an angle to handle any trouble that came along. But Jess wasn't around any more. Jess was dead. And this trouble, now staring him squarely in the eye, was the biggest trouble Hoke had ever faced. His crippled shoulder was giving him pure hell, and what these teamsters were promising. . . .

Sash Perkins moved over and stared down at Hoke and there was a loathing and blank hatred in Sash's eyes that made Hoke squirm. "You dirty whelp!" gritted Sash. "Damned if I can figger how anything like you ever managed to get on this earth. But for some reason the Lord made vermin that crawls on its belly or walks on four legs, so I guess some that walks on two legs managed to slip by. But we got a remedy for your kind. You take and mix a stout tree limb and a length of rope with a noose in one end, and then a long drop!"

Hoke stared back at Sash, but his eyes went blank and unseeing, his thoughts frantic. *Jess, where are you? Jess, how'll I get out of this?*

The door of the bunkhouse opened and Clay Roswell came in. He'd had something to eat and a few hours' sleep. He could have used a lot more, but the worst edge had been taken off the grinding fatigue that had weighted his shoulders. Sash Perkins turned to him.

"Here's your man, Clay. I told you I'd see to it that he didn't make a wiggle. How about gettin' this thing over with? The boys got the rope ready and we know the tree."

"We'll get to that in a minute, Sash," Clay answered. "But maybe Pickard has got something he'd like to say. How about it, Pickard? You and Jess didn't handle those two raids by yourselves. You had somebody else to help you drive the wagons. While we're at it, we aim to make a clean sweep of the gang."

Hoke Pickard swung his head from side to side, like some trapped and desperate animal. But he did not answer. Clay turned to the teamsters, shrugged. "Let's go!"

A teamster pushed up. "Here's the rope. I can't wait to pull on it. Danny Huggins and Brad Lincoln, I'll be thinking of them."

Hoke Pickard stared at the rope as though it were a coiled rattlesnake, ready to strike. The muscles of his throat worked spasmodically.

"Just you and me, Roswell," he mumbled. "If I talk, do I get a break?"

Instantly an angry yell went up from the teamsters. "No deal with that whelp. He swings!"

Clay quieted them with an upraised hand. "I'm not promising you a thing, Hoke. Not a thing beyond this. I don't know what kind of authorized law there is here in Fort Churchill, if any. But what there is, I'll let you take your chances with. It may hang you anyhow. But that's the best I can do."

Hoke's throat worked again. There was no chance with these teamsters, he could see that. There never was any hope with a group of righteously angry men bent on vigilante action. The history of this Western frontier had proven that time and again. But there might be a thin chance otherwise.

"I'll take that chance." Hoke gulped. "Get this crowd out of here and I'll talk."

Again the teamsters protested, but Clay cut them off curtly. "Get outside, boys! I want to hear what this fellow has to say. No argument. Outside!"

They went finally, protesting. Clay closed the door, turned back. "All right. Start talking."

Hoke had to clear his throat. "Jess and me, we had three others helpin' us. By name, Jackson, Schwartz, and Early. Just three wagon bums we picked up who needed a few dollars and wasn't no way squeamish about how they got 'em. All they did was help swap loads and drive the smaller wagons where we wanted them. Then we paid them off and right now I'm damned if I know where you'd find them. Probably layin' around somewheres drunk."

"That's damned small help," rapped Clay harshly. "Not worth saving your neck over. There's more, a lot more, and that's what I want. Let's have it!"

"You'll think different about the rest of it," retorted Hoke. "Raidin' those freight outfits wasn't Jess's or my idea to begin with. We were workin' for somebody else, on shares. This'll set you on your heels, Roswell . . . but it's the truth, so help me."

There had been little enough resistance to fear in Hoke to begin with. Now that little was rapidly running out of him.

Once having started to talk, he couldn't get rid of the words fast enough. They fell from his working lips almost feverishly.

Cold contempt swept through Clay Roswell. With a club to swing in the dark of night on an unsuspecting victim, or free to work his knife in a barroom brawl, Hoke Pickard was dangerous, and ruthless perhaps. But now, with the cards all down and falling against him, the man was a cringing coward.

Clay knew another emotion besides the contempt he felt. It was a cold thing, hitting at him deep, because he felt that he knew what Hoke was going to say next and, though the thought itself had been hovering in the back of Clay's mind, because of the implications it would carry, he was now reluctant to hear it laid out in the spoken word. Yet—he had to know. His tone went bleak.

"All right. Let's have the rest of it."

Hoke drew a deep breath. "The man Jess and me were working for is Reed Owen."

There it was! That was it. The thing Clay knew he was going to hear, yet dreaded. And because he had to make very sure of this damning disclosure, he tried to throw the words back in Hoke's teeth.

"Reed Owen? You're lying and you know it. Reed Owen is one of Jack Casement's right-hand men. He's got Casement's full confidence. I tell you I want the truth, not crazy lies."

"I'm givin' you the truth," vowed Hoke stubbornly. "I'm givin' it to you exactly straight. Maybe Owen is one of Casement's trusted men. But that's just the angle that Owen figgers to cash in on. Listen. Who do you think owns that Bear Wallow Flat trading post? Bib Henry? Like hell. Reed Owen owns it. And he owns the one at Myers Wells, out in the desert. And he owns the one at Sugar Pine, higher up than Bear Wallow in the mountains. Mebbe he owns more of them along the trail. I dunno about that. But I'm damn' sure he owns the three

I told you. And if you don't believe me, all you got to do to find
out is nose around any one of them places long enough. If you'd
have put more pressure on Bib Henry at Bear Wallow, he'd have
told you who owned the place. It belongs to Reed Owen, and
that's no lie. Now here's somethin' else."

Hoke broke off, coughed a little before starting on again in
that feverish, hurried way.

"Why d'you think Reed Owen tried so hard to sell Jack Casement on the idea of hirin' Jess and me as wagon bosses? He
did, you know. He was tryin' to get Casement to agree to that
the day in the Shoshone Bar when you came in and jumped
Jess and me. And why did he want us for wagon bosses? Because
that would have made it easier for him to have got his hands on
wagonloads of supplies he aimed to steal and sell at a big profit
in his trading posts."

There was no stopping Hoke now, for he felt that he was
arguing for his neck and he was doing it desperately.

"Another thing. Didn't you have a row with Owen the day
before the jump-off . . . a row over a wagon overloaded with
flour? Who tried to overload it? Reed Owen did. And why?
Because that was a load of flour we aimed to steal that night,
and did steal, and Owen wanted to get as much on it as he
could. Now you add all those things up, Roswell, and see if you
still think I'm lyin'."

Hoke settled back on the bunk, breathing hard.

No, thought Clay somberly, Hoke wasn't lying. He was just
speaking all the things that had been running around in Clay's
mind and they made a pattern that no man could fail to
recognize.

Clay got out his pipe, made a turn up and down the room.
Hoke watched him intently, trying to read what was going on
behind the taciturn bleakness that pulled Clay's face into hard
and bitter lines. Hoke tried some more.

"Reed Owen hates your guts, don't he, Roswell? Right from the first, didn't he? Why? Because you blew up his scheme to get me and Jess on as wagon bosses. Because you backed him down on overloadin' that wagon. Because he knows damn' well you don't trust him like Jack Casement does, and that makes him afraid of you. He'd like nothin' better than to get a slug between your shoulders some dark night. Oh, I tell you Reed Owen has got some big ideas for himself. He knows that wire-stringin' job ain't goin' to last forever and by the time it's done he aims to have himself set up in the tradin' business in fine style . . . on somebody else's money. Oh, an ambitious feller, Reed Owen."

"Enough of that," said Clay harshly. "Who actually killed Brad Lincoln and Danny Huggins?"

His glance bored at Hoke as he asked this and he saw Hoke's eyes waver and grow shifty. Hoke licked his lips, then gave blurting answer: "Jess did. Jess killed them both. I told him it wasn't necessary to go that far. I told him. . . ."

"Shut up!" Clay stood over Hoke with blazing eyes. "Now I know you're lying. You never in your life worried about a man being killed. Don't try and make me believe that. Maybe Jess did kill those two men . . . and maybe he didn't. Maybe you did. But Jess is dead and can't tell his side. You'd try and save your worthless neck by heaping blame on a dead man . . . on your own brother."

Clay swung away, half sickened with disgust. This fellow, Hoke Pickard. How low could a man crawl when abject cowardice had him by the throat? If there was an atom of remorse or grief in Hoke over the fact that his brother was dead, he didn't show it; he was concerned only with himself. And if he held any hate for Clay, the man who had killed his brother, it was now completely submerged by his craven eagerness to save his own neck. These things were enough to sicken anyone. Clay headed for the door.

"You promised!" Hoke shrilled after him. "Remember . . . you promised!"

At the door Clay paused, looked back. "Yeah," he said thickly, "I promised I'd try and locate some established authority to turn you over to. I promised that and I'll do my best. But if I locate that authority, I still hope it hangs you."

Clay opened the door and stepped out. Sash Perkins and the other teamsters were waiting. Clay spoke wearily.

"Your chore now, Sash. Keep an eye on Pickard and see that nobody bothers him. I promised him that, if he'd talk, he'd get his chance with established authority. I intend to see that he does. Now I'm off to try and locate that authority."

"So he talked, eh?" said Sash. "What did he have to say? Who killed Brad Lincoln and . . . ?"

Clay shook his head. "That doesn't matter now." He walked away, heading uptown, before more questions were thrown at him. For how could he answer any of them without disclosing the part Reed Owen played in this villainy? And he had no right to spread that. Right now he didn't know what he was going to do about it.

Sash Perkins set himself in the bunkhouse door, blocking it when the other teamsters would have pushed through.

"No go now, boys," said Sash. "Hands off! Me, I'm just as anxious as the rest of you are to see that damned whelp inside strung up. But Clay made some sort of deal with him and gave him a promise, so this thing will have to be worked out the way Clay says. Remember, it was Clay who ran this deal down and brought Pickard in. Yeah, it's Clay's cat and it's goin' to be skinned the way Clay wants it."

A brawny young teamster with sea-blue eyes and wheat-yellow hair showed a hard grin. "Now that's tellin' us, Sash, and being a good boy. You're a good feller and we all like you. We like Clay, too. But it sure goes against the grain to think of a damn' sneak thief and killer in the night like that Pickard is, havin' even the slightest chance of wigglin' free, which he may do unless we make sure. So, give a hand, Jake!"

With the words, the brawny young muleskinner dived at Sash, driving a hard-muscled shoulder into Sash's middle, slamming Sash up against the doorpost. Before Sash could recover, the young teamster had hold of him and instantly there were all the rest to help.

Sash cursed and fought. He got a clenched fist home to the young teamster's face, and the blue-eyed one's grin only widened.

"Purty good for you, Sash, but not good enough. You're stout, but not stout enough to do for all of us. So take it easy and no hard feelin's. Remember, us fellers didn't make no deal or give no promises to anybody. Now quit your damned ruckus or I'll have to get you down and sit on you."

Sash still did the best he could, but he had no chance against this bunch of determined men. He knew them all—they were all his friends. But now they muscled him down, carried him inside, and tied him to a bunk. And then they moved over to Hoke Pickard who saw what was in their faces and went completely broken.

"That damned Roswell!" Hoke raved. "He lied to me! He made me his promise and now . . . !"

The blue-eyed one jammed a hard palm against Hoke's mouth. "Enough of that squallin'. Clay Roswell didn't lie to you. He spoke for himself and he's off to do what he can for you now. But he didn't speak for us and we're damned sure what we're goin' to do."

Hoke would have fought if he could, for there was a rat-like terror cutting all through him. But his wounded shoulder hampered him and these teamsters were strong and bitterly set on what they were going to do, and there was no stopping them. Hoke got his mouth free and began to beg. "A chance . . . gimme a chance . . . !"

"Like the chance you gave Brad Lincoln and Danny Huggins, I suppose?" came the blue-eyed one's hard, answering growl. "All right, boys. We can't risk the time and we don't need a tree. That rafter joist yonder is strong enough. Where's that rope? Get it done!"

Sash Perkins had to lie there and watch it. And that rafter joist creaked and creaked to the spinning, writhing weight that swung to it, creaked like it might if a chill and grisly wind had suddenly begun to blow and buffet the whole building.

After it was done with, and the rafter no longer creaked, they untied Sash and the blue-eyed one said: "Now you better go hunt up Clay Roswell and tell him about it, Sash. Tell him not to be sore at us. But this was somethin' we just had to do, and we did it."

They tramped out, and Sash, after one more look around, followed them.

Chapter Twelve

Over at the Pony Express headquarters, Alex Majors walked into an office momentarily empty, settled himself at his desk, lit up the first cheroot of the day, and made ready for another day of work. Came a step at the office door and Majors peered through a cloud of tobacco smoke. Recognition flickered in his keen eyes and a quick, warm smile pulled at his bearded lips.

"Roswell. How are you, lad? Glad to see you again." He stretched a hearty hand across his desk.

Over the handclasp, Clay said: "It's good to see you, too, sir. Wonder if you could spare me a few minutes?"

"Of course. You're looking mighty fit. Been hearing things about you . . . good things. Hear that you're doing a fine job as Casement's wagon boss. Now that was a good hunch I had, sending you out to see Casement that day you came to me looking for a job."

"Yes, sir, it was." Clay nodded. "And I'll always be obliged to you for that."

Majors waved the thanks aside. "You wouldn't have made the job in the first place, and then held it, if you didn't have the stuff in you." Majors's eyes turned keen. "Something you wanted to ask me?"

Clay nodded again. "I'll make it as brief as possible. Here it is, sir."

He went on then to sketch the story of the raided wagons, how he'd run down the trail as far as Bear Wallow, and of what had taken place out there. Majors listened intently and with obvious interest, making one small, growled remark. "The dirty scum. They deserve to be hung."

"That's just the problem, sir," went on Clay. "I knew that the Pickards couldn't have handled things alone, so to find out who else was mixed in, I had to get this Hoke Pickard to talk. And to do that I had to offer him the chance to settle his future with some constituted authority. That's what I came to you about, mainly. Can you tell me if there is any such constituted authority here at Fort Churchill, and, if there is, where I'll find it?"

Alex Majors leaned back in his chair. "There's supposed to be a façade of law in existence here at Churchill, son, but from what I've seen of it, it's a sketchy and uncertain thing at best. Actually, though it might seem otherwise to the first casual glance, there isn't any real permanency to Fort Churchill, as the future will prove when Jack Casement has finished his wire-stringing job and we of the Express have pulled up stakes. The time will come when Fort Churchill will be nothing but a half-forgotten dot on a map. People won't stop in Churchill. They'll just be moving through it, one way or another. Everybody realizes that, so that is why no real attempt has been made to set up a solid fabric of constituted law."

Majors's cheroot had gone out and now he paused to freshen it again. "Another thing. What law there is here at the moment stops at the limits of Churchill. The bulk of your trouble, it seems, took place well beyond Churchill, so that throws the whole thing into another light. I confess I don't know just where or how you're going to find the authority to handle this thing. Now would it be any real loss if your teamsters went ahead and lynched this fellow, Pickard?"

"None in the least, sir," said Clay. "Only . . . I gave him my promise."

"And he talked?"

"Yes, he talked."

Majors did not miss the somberness of Clay's tone and look. "And you heard things that weren't pleasant?" Majors asked.

"I heard things that I still don't know just how to handle, sir," said Clay. "I heard things that are going to hurt Jack Casement very badly. Men he trusted fully. . . ."

"Ah," said Alex Majors, "that I can fully understand. I've had it happen to me, more than once. There's always some it seems, and I agree it's a wicked jolt." He puffed a moment savagely, spurred by old memories. Then in a tone mildly kind: "Don't let it get you down, son. After all, that sort of thing is more Casement's problem than it is yours. You got things to tell Casement, why then you go ahead and tell him, even if it sets off some fireworks. Casement is a big enough man to take that sort of disappointment and move on past it. In the end he'll thank you."

There was an apologetic cough at the door of the office. Sash Perkins stood there. At sight of him, Clay showed a quick flash of anger.

"Sash, I thought I told you to stay with Hoke Pickard."

"Yeah, you did," admitted Sash. He moved a couple of steps in from the door. "Been trying to find you, Clay. Feller told me he saw you come in here." Sash paused to draw a deep breath, then went on with a swift rush of words. "I stood guard at the door of the bunkhouse. I wouldn't let any of the other boys go in. All of a sudden, without any warnin', they jumped me. I fought the best I could, but there was too many of them. They hauled me inside and tied me on a bunk. They wasn't mad at me. They just knew what they intended to do, and they went ahead and did it. They said that, while you might have made a deal with Hoke Pickard and given him some kind of promise, they hadn't done either. So then they grabbed Hoke and they hung him to a rafter joist and . . . and . . . well, I guess that's it."

Clay went very still and the anger in his eyes slowly died, leaving a gray bitterness. Sash shifted uneasily. "The boys said they hoped you wouldn't be mad at them. They was just afraid that Hoke might have some way skinned through clear, unless they made sure he didn't." Sash shifted uneasy feet again.

Clay's head came up. "All right, Sash. You and I . . . we did our best. Wait for me outside."

Sash ducked out, obvious relief in his face. Clay turned to Alex Majors again. "I guess that's part of the problem taken care of, sir. It made me out a liar, but I can't blame the men too much."

"I wouldn't blame them at all, son," said Alex Majors flatly. "And you weren't made out a liar. You were doing your best to keep your promise to that fellow, Pickard. What happened was beyond your control. And I can't think of a better answer. From what you told me of Hoke Pickard, he was headed for a rope somewhere, eventually. Now it's over and done with. In your boots I wouldn't have a single regret. You know, son, there's something about a dose of real, old-fashioned frontier justice that clears the air like nothing else can. It sort of puts a period to things. Now you can go ahead with the rest of the job."

"I guess you're right, sir. Thanks for your time and advice. I feel better."

Alex Majors stood up to shake hands this time. "You're more than welcome. I tell you I was glad to see you. Drop around any time and let me know how that wire job is going. Good luck, son."

Sash Perkins was waiting a few strides outside the door. Clay dropped a hand on his shoulder. "It's all right, Sash. No hard feelings. Now, here is what you do. First, you round up those wild devils who took care of Hoke Pickard and tell them that, as long as they hung him, it's up to them to bury him. Then you hook up a wagon and team and head out for Bear Wallow Flat. You won't need one of the big outfits . . . a medium rig will do. At Bear Wallow you look up a fellow named Blaine . . . Jim Blaine. He'll show you where that stolen flour of ours is, there in the trading post. Haul it back to our warehouse. Then you hit your regular wagon route again. See you out at point of wire. That's where I'm heading."

CHAPTER THIRTEEN

Despite the comforting viewpoint that Alex Majors had offered him, that gray bitterness of mood came back to Clay Roswell as he jogged down the long desert and mountain miles to the east. Not because a renegade killer had been lynched, but because of certain things he knew he must tell to certain people.

There was just no way of dodging this. The things he had learned had to be told and acted on, no matter who was hurt. For it wasn't a thing you could carry with you and keep covered up. The entire success of the big job could conceivably depend on this—on the truth being made known. And there was only one way of rightly curing matters. Alex Majors was completely right there. It had to be done by Jack Casement.

It was up to him to carry the word to Casement. He felt he knew Jack Casement well enough by this time to understand how Casement felt toward his friends and toward those in whom he'd placed his full trust. It was going to be rough on Casement.

But, rough as it would be for Casement to take, how would it be for Katherine Casement? There was no doubting her friendship with Reed Owen. Clay had observed enough to understand that. Whether a deeper emotion than mere friendship existed between the two, Clay couldn't be sure. But most certainly a degree of fondness was there. And so, in that quarter, this thing could leave a wound that would be deep and long-lived. In the drive of the work ahead, Jack Casement could in time undoubtedly put the disillusionment behind him. But Jack Casement's daughter—what of her? How long could a woman's memory run?

The miles were long, the sun's heat fierce and unrelenting, and the weight of his thoughts bowed Clay's head and shoulders. He rode the miles out in a sort of mental and physical stupor.

These crews of Jack Casement's, these groups of shaggy, sweating, toiling men—they had crossed Cedar Springs Pass and gone down the other side, leaving in their wake that unbroken line of striding poles and the graceful swoops of wire that sang in the wind and glittered in the sun's brightness. Now they were planting more poles and stringing more wire along the twisting miles of a long running valley to the east that spread its narrow flatness between rounded, brooding slopes masked with gray and silent sage. Miles on to the east, softened by distance, another gaunt and mist-smoked mountain backbone waited to battle them with hidden defile and craggy shoulder.

Certain supplies still had to be brought in over the ever-lengthening miles from Fort Churchill, and so the path of progress was still marked by long, low banners of dust where the big freighters and strings of toiling mules creaked and plodded. But the pole wagons had it easier now, hauling from the newly cut supply in the timber stands to the east of Cedar Springs Pass.

Riding in, Clay Roswell was startled at the progress that had been made in the few short days he'd been away. This sprawling, strung-out mixture of men and wagons and mules was a machine geared to greater efficiency than seemed apparent at first glance.

Midafternoon's heat lay in a breathless blanket across this lonely wilderness valley when Clay came up with Jack Casement's headquarters wagon. Casement and Tom Hughes, of the survey gang, were studying some survey maps and figures that were spread out on an upturned box in the scanty shade offered by a tarpaulin stretched from the side of the wagon and supported at the outer corners by stakes driven into the ground.

Tom Hughes began rolling up the maps and Jack Casement turned and scrubbed a shirt sleeve across a sweating face as Clay reined in and dismounted. Clay's face was dark with sun and unshaven whisker stubble, and he was gray with the dust of travel. He moved a little stiffly as he walked. His eyes were shadowed and he reflected a taciturn somberness.

In Jack Casement's eyes lay that same burning brilliance of undiminished energy and electric drive, and there was a shade of sternness in his tone as he spoke.

"Well, here you are finally. By the looks of you you've done plenty of traveling. I hope the results justified it?"

Clay understood what lay behind Casement's tone and definite stiffness of manner. Casement wasn't entirely pleased over the fact that Clay had taken it upon himself to leave the main job without permission or consultation. A faint tinge of color swept across Clay's fatigue-pulled cheeks.

"I struck a good trail and I didn't want to leave it while it was hot," he explained quietly. "As far as keeping the wagons rolling, Bill Yerkes could handle that chore just as good or better than I could. I didn't figure to be missed too much. And, yes, I think the results more than justified what I did."

Tom Hughes, tall and lank and tough as sun-cured rawhide, realizing that this was something that did not concern him, tramped away with long, swinging strides. At the same time there was a rustle in the wagon and Katherine Casement came climbing down from under its canvas top, bringing some paperwork and progress books with her. Even in this flat, still heat she still managed a cool, crisp look. Clay touched his hat to her, then looked at Jack Casement again.

"The story isn't a pretty one, Mister Casement."

Casement's tone still held that note of curtness: "Kitts is old enough to listen. Whatever it is, it can't be much worse than what we had to face last night. Two of our survey gang were caught out alone by some Goshiutes. When we missed them and went looking for them and found them and brought them in, they didn't even resemble the human beings they had been. All right, let's have your story, Roswell. I know that a teamster named Huggins, along with his outfit, disappeared somewhere on the road between here and Fort Churchill. You went looking for him. What did you find?"

"Why, first," said Clay, "I found Danny Huggins lying in one of those little sand valleys at the foot of the mountain west of Cedar Springs Pass. He was dead . . . shot. Then I found his wagon and mules a couple of miles to the north. The wagon, of course, was empty. The thieves had handled things just the way they did with Skip Keswick's wagon. They had switched the load to several lighter wagons, which had gone farther north from there to turn in on the main emigrant trail. There was no chance of trailing these wagons, so I picked up Huggins's body and drove his wagon back to Churchill. From there I headed out for the Sierras."

"And what did you expect to find out there?" demanded Casement.

"Just what I did find. Ever since the affair of Brad Lincoln's death and the theft of Skip Keswick's wagon, I've been trying to figure out some answers. One of these seemed pretty sound to me. For instance, a hungry man wouldn't steal a wagonload of flour. He might try and get away with a barrel or two, but not a wagonload, for, if he was figuring on it for his own use, a barrel or maybe two would be all he'd think of. So, it seemed to me that whoever stole the stuff, must be figuring on selling it somewhere. The best answer to that, as I saw it, lay in some of the smaller supply posts along the emigrant route. So I decided

I'd check up on a couple of them."

Casement nodded, a little grudgingly. "Logical reasoning. Go on."

"I stopped at our warehouse first," said Clay. "I wanted to find out if there was any particular identifying mark on the flour barrels we used. It turned out that there was, for, while Abbott and Ives flour is in pretty general use on this side of the mountains, each barrel we store in our warehouse is marked by a cross in crayon as it is counted off an incoming load from Sacramento. So that gave me something to go on."

"I suppose Reed Owen pointed that out to you?" said Casement.

Clay shook his head, his eyes inscrutable. "Owen wasn't there. A warehouse hand showed me how it was done. Well, at Bear Wallow Flat I found what I was looking for. Some of our stolen flour was there. The crayoned cross had been scraped off the barrels with a knife, but that left its own mark. A fellow named Bib Henry was running the trading post. I went in first, acting like I wanted to buy some flour. This fellow Bib Henry's asking price was a hundred and fifty dollars a barrel. Quite a chunk of profit there from a wagonload of stolen flour, don't you think?"

A little of the stiffness began to leave Casement's manner. His eyes were gleaming with quickening interest. "Profit indeed," he rapped. "Go on."

"When I began questioning this fellow Bib Henry, he got a little shifty and evasive. I had to throw my gun on him. I made him tell me where he got the flour. He said he'd bought it off two brothers . . . the Pickards."

That really hit Jack Casement. "The Pickards. I'll be damned. What next?"

"Well," said Clay, "this Bib Henry tried to catch me off guard and manhandle me. I had to cool him off with my gun barrel. Right after that, who should drive up to the post in a light

wagon loaded with more of our stolen flour, but those same two
brothers, Jess and Hoke Pickard."

Katherine Casement had been listening to all this with a
grave, but deep interest. Clay touched her with a brief glance
before going on, his voice gruff.

"Things went pretty wild and rough, then. The second he
recognized me, Jess Pickard went for his gun. I killed him. I had
no other out. It was him or me. Hoke Pickard dragged a rifle
out of the wagon, so I had to use my gun on him, too. I crippled
his shoulder. I had to do some explaining to the fellow who
runs the stage station at Bear Wallow . . . by name of Jim Blaine.
He said he knew you. I convinced him of the truth of my side of
the affair and he agreed to keep an eye on the flour in the trading post until I could send a man up for it. That has been done.
I drove the Pickard wagon and its load back to Fort Churchill
myself, and turned the flour in at our warehouse. I still didn't
see Reed Owen around. I also brought Hoke Pickard back to
Churchill with me."

"That's more than I'd have done," burst out Casement with
startling savagery. "The damned, murdering thief. I'd have left
him right there with his brother Jess, and just as dead."

Clay shrugged. "It stood to reason that there was somebody
else in the mess besides the Pickards and that fellow Bib Henry.
I figured maybe I could get Hoke Pickard to talk if I put the
right kind of pressure on him. It was a good guess. With a
noosed rope looking him in the eye, he did talk . . . and plenty.
I promised I'd give him a break if he gave me the information I
wanted, and I intended to. But a bunch of our teamsters who
knew Brad Lincoln and Danny Huggins felt differently. I left
Sash Perkins to guard Hoke Pickard. These other teamsters
caught Sash off guard, jumped him, tied him up, then lynched
Hoke Pickard."

Clay glanced at Katherine Casement again as he said this

and he saw her lips tighten a little and the pallor of shock faintly touch her face. This sort of business was rough for a girl to listen to. But Jack Casement apparently never gave that a thought. His voice was a hard growl.

"Damned good riddance. An Indian renegade along the trail is bad enough. But a white one . . . he's worse. What was it that this fellow Hoke Pickard told you? Did he name anybody else in that rotten gang?"

Clay pushed a hand across his eyes. Now it came. This was the moment he'd been dreading. He nodded woodenly. "Yes. Yes, he did. This is going to jolt you . . . plenty, Mister Casement."

Clay could feel the girl's eyes upon him and Casement was staring at him between pinched lids. "Why jolt me?" Casement demanded. "Is it that you're suggesting that one of our own men was working with the Pickards? That we've a damned traitor among us? Is that it?"

"That's it."

"Name him," exploded Casement. "Name him, and I'll see to it that there's another lynching!"

Clay squared his shoulders, set his jaw, and met Casement's boring glance fully and steadily.

"Very well, Mister Casement. Here it is. That man is . . . Reed Owen."

For a long moment there was a silence thick enough to cut. Then there was a little hissing intake of breath from Katherine Casement and a sharp cry.

"That's a lie! That's a contemptible lie! Dad . . . !"

Jack Casement had rocked up on his toes and his voice rang harshly. "Quiet, Kitts!" He surged toward Clay, his eyes stormy with anger. "Roswell, do you realize what you're saying . . . what you're asking me to believe?"

"Yes," said Clay steadily. "I do. And if you think I've enjoyed the realization that I had to tell you this, think again. But it's what Hoke Pickard told me . . . and it adds up."

Careless of her father's admonition, Katherine Casement came pressing in between him and Clay Roswell. She faced Clay with blazing eyes.

"I know you've never liked Reed," she flamed. "I've seen that from the first. But if you think you can come behind his back like this, that you can undermine him and gain favor by . . . by . . . ! Oh, I never heard a more despicable lie."

Clay knew it was useless to try and reason with this furious girl. So he looked past her and held Jack Casement's glance.

"You," said Casement, suddenly quiet, almost dangerously so, "you'd better be able to prove what you're saying, Roswell. For if you can't. . . . I've known Reed Owen a long time. I trust him implicitly. He's been the best supply boss I ever had working for me. So now, I want some proof to back up your words. Where is it?"

"I'll give it to you as Hoke Pickard gave it to me," said Clay. "Reed Owen is the real owner of the trading posts at Myers Wells, at Bear Wallow Flat, and Sugar Pine. There may be others, along the emigrant route. Reed Owen has ideas of being a merchant prince on this side of the Sierras after this wire-stringing job is done. And he figures to set himself up on someone else's money. There it is."

Despite the grip of her father's hands on her shoulders, trying to put her aside, Katherine Casement was not to be quieted.

"The word of this . . . this Hoke Pickard," she stormed. "A self-confessed murderer and thief. On the word of such a person you'd try and blacken Reed Owen to Dad and me. What kind of a man are you, Clay Roswell?"

"Kitts has got something there, Roswell," growled Casement. "The word of a rat like Hoke Pickard isn't enough to satisfy me, not near enough. I can't see how it is with you, either. I thought you had better judgment than that."

Suddenly, out of nowhere, anger flamed through Clay Roswell. He'd put so much into this thing, gambled his own life to some extent, and felt that he was doing the right thing by Casement and by the job. And now they were tossing the lie into his face. The gray of his eyes grew smoky, turned dark.

"So that's the way it is, eh?" he rapped harshly. "Well, now . . . maybe I've been a damned fool for even bothering my head about the whole thing. I think I have been. Let 'em murder our men, steal our supplies. We don't want any of the truth of the thing because it's unpleasant. Because it makes a traitor and a thief out of Reed Owen. Well, as long as I've gone this far, I'll have my whole say and then head for other parts."

He held Casement with the bitterest of glances. "Why do you think, Casement, that Reed Owen was so anxious to get you to hire on the Pickards to boss your wagons? He was, wasn't he? Believe I heard you admit that yourself. Why was he so friendly with the Pickards? Why did he act real put out when you hired me for the job and turned down the Pickards? Or maybe you've forgotten that. And then there was an argument the afternoon before the jump-off, an argument about an overloaded wagon . . . overloaded with flour. Skip Keswick's wagon. Which was stolen with its full load, that night. Could it have been that Reed Owen knew that wagon and its load was to be run off and so he wanted all the flour in that particular wagon he could possibly pile there? Ask your daughter about that argument . . . she was there."

Jack Casement was no fool. With the first shock of Clay's charge wearing off, and with the logic of Clay's angry words pounding at him, some of the bristle went out of him and a harried, anxious look began to show in his eyes.

"Yeah," Clay surged on. "Think of all those things like I have. Sure it's a dirty, ugly picture. But facts are facts. And I might add that the evening after the argument about the overloaded wagon, and the evening before Brad Lincoln was clubbed to death and that same wagon stolen, I saw the Pickards and Reed Owen together in town, going off real chummy. It didn't take you long to read the Pickards for what they were, Casement. So why should Owen have been so blind, unless willfully so? No, I don't like Reed Owen. Your daughter is right there. I've never liked him, from the first. His eyes are too damned hard and shifty. And then he used his fist on little Skip Keswick without reasonable cause . . . on Skip, who isn't more than two-thirds his size. I don't like men like that."

Clay drew a deep breath, then went on more quietly.

"So now you know. What I've done was not done with the idea of deliberately blackening Reed Owen or anybody else. I don't give a thin damn about Reed Owen. I've tried to do what I thought was right by you and the job and myself. Now, if you want to call me a liar for it, I'll take the word from you . . . once. Aside from that I'm done, right now. I'm going to gather up my blankets and other gear, and then you can pay me off. I guess that says everything."

Clay turned away, stepped into his saddle, and sent his horse whipping off.

The stillness in Jack Casement deepened. But the girl was still shaking with anger. Casement's grip on her shoulders tightened.

"Steady, Kitts," he said slowly. "Steady. I . . . I don't think you and I handled things very well just now. Steady."

She turned. "Dad, you're not saying you believe this? Oh, Dad, you couldn't believe that against . . . Reed?"

"Child," said Jack Casement, "this is as stiff a jolt as I ever had to take in my life. Everything in me is saying that it just can't be. Yet . . . what reason would Clay Roswell have for lying? What . . . ?"

"Because he hates Reed!" broke in the girl fiercely. "He admits he does. And. . . ."

"No, you're wrong there," said Casement, shaking his head. "Maybe Roswell does hate Reed, but that isn't the reason he's brought this word to us. He isn't that kind. He earnestly believes every word he spoke. We must remember that Clay Roswell has served my interests and those of the company faithfully. He has done so at plenty of personal risk to himself. He's worked out a wicked trail of murder and thievery, and just because that trail leads to an answer neither of us wants to accept is no reason for us to turn on him as we have. This thing has got to be investigated and the truth pinned down, no matter who it touches and who it hurts. So I'm going to start that investigation now. I'm going to run down the truth, one way or another."

He put the girl aside and hurried away in the direction Clay Roswell had ridden. He had luck in finding, not too far along, Clay talking to Bill Yerkes, both of them stoic and sober of face. Clay stood taciturn and expressionless as Casement came up to them. It was not Jack Casement's way to beat around the bush.

"Perhaps I was hasty back there, Roswell. I think I was. For a time there you had me off balance. Now here is what I propose to do. I know where Myers Wells is. It's north of here, a fair distance. It will be well after dark when we get there. But I'm asking you to ride up there with me. I want to see with my own eyes what supplies they got there. And I want to ask some damn' straight questions of whoever is in charge there. Well?"

Clay considered for a moment. Then he nodded and answered gruffly: "All right. I'm with you."

CHAPTER FOURTEEN

The desert night lay all around them. They had come out of the mountains, angling toward the north and west, and here the going was easier, and they hit the regular emigrant route and rode back along it. Little had passed between them on the way and little passed between them now, each riding with his own thoughts.

They were thoughts weighted with trouble. Somber conviction strengthened and grew in Jack Casement. He was a man torn between the wish not to believe and a stubborn and damning array of circumstances that demanded that he must believe. A man trained to accomplish concrete things, he knew there was no substitute for facts, and in this matter there seemed to be many of them. Several times as he rode he sighed deeply.

As for Clay Roswell, he rode in a sort of locked taciturnity of mood that left him empty and cold inside. Because all taste of the future was gone. Although he had not shown it openly, there had lived within him in the past weeks a fine, great enthusiasm for the big job, an enthusiasm and satisfaction that had grown with every mile of advance.

It had been as Alex Majors had told him it would be. To be even a small part of an undertaking that would go down in history would give a man a satisfaction and inner reward that he could hold to and cherish all the rest of his life. It would be a prop to a man's self-esteem and a solid rock of confidence that could hold a man up to any other job he might face in all his later years. It would be a sort of hallmark of ability and courage.

That was the way it had been with Clay. But no more. All the flavor of it was gone. The feeling was on him now that he didn't give a damn. They could string wires or they could let it lay. In any event, he was through. He was making this ride with Casement for just one purpose—to prove his point. That done—well, he'd head on west and see what lay on the far side of the brooding Sierras.

Deep inside he still writhed as he recalled the scene of that afternoon at the headquarters wagon. The way they had so flatly flung the lie into his face. He had expected a shocked reaction, but not that flat and scathing disbelief. He had given a lot of himself to running down this thing. He had felt the breath of hostile lead and he had shot a man to death. He had whipped himself physically, going without food or sleep. He had garnered facts beyond argument, and then it had all been thrown back in his face as a lie.

It seemed he could still see Katherine Casement, standing there before him, coppery head back, blue eyes blazing her anger and contempt, while she whipped him with words of scorn. Well, if he'd wanted proof of her real feelings toward Reed Owen, he certainly had them now. For she had defended Owen almost savagely.

Which, come to think of it, meant another dream gone to hell. It had been a shy, hesitant dream, locked deep inside him, but it had been a good one. Come to think of it, it had been a large part of the reason he'd put so much drive and enthusiasm into his part of the big job, the idea of accomplishment to lay before Katherine Casement for her approval. His lips twisted in silent derision. Now what a damned fool fancy that had been!

The desert was a silver mist of translucent star shine all about them. It was a light in which a man saw things that weren't there and did not see things that were. Only one thing could a man be sure of—here was a lonely and empty land. And with a perversity all its own, this high desert that could be such a cauldron of heat in the daytime, at night could know a biting chill. That chill was there now, and, as he rode, Clay hunched his shoulders against the bite of it.

A faint pinpoint of light lifted ahead and Jack Casement spoke for the first time in long miles. "There it is. Myers Wells."

A small feeling of uncertainty took hold of Clay Roswell. What if they found no incriminating evidence at this place? That was entirely possible. Perhaps none of the stolen flour had been hauled out here. Maybe all of it had been taken to Bear Wallow and Sugar Pine and other trading posts higher and deeper into the Sierras. That would leave him high and dry in his accusations against Reed Owen. If Jack Casement hadn't believed before, he certainly wouldn't believe now.

Clay shook aside the uncertainty. The hell with it. He knew what he knew. And someday Casement would know, too. So, for that matter, would Katherine.

There were two low and ragged backbones of rock, lifting grayly out of a gray desert, reaching out from a common point in a sort of rough V. Deep in the angle laid the water. Not very good water, with the bite of alkali in it—yet, water. And in the mouth of the V, squatting there as though guarding the water beyond, was the low, crude building that was the trading post.

Off to one side of the post a couple of gaunt Conestoga emigrant wagons were drawn up and there was a small stir of life around them. A small glow lay flat against the earth, where a campfire had burned and had sifted down to only a few small ruby embers, dusted with ash and fading out. A thread of wood smoke coiled in invisibility but laid its acrid touch against a man's nostrils.

Yellow light shone feebly through a lone open window of the

post, as though cowering and timorous against the vastness of the desert night.

Their horses sagged to a weary halt, and they swung down. Jack Casement stood for a moment, stamping some feeling into his stiffened legs. He wasn't toughened up to saddle work like Clay was. Casement went to the door and, without knocking, pushed it open. Clay moved in beside him, wary and alert.

There was a table with a couple of benches beside it. A rough counter ran along one wall with several shelves beyond it, stacked with supplies of one sort and another. Deeper in the place were the heavier and more bulky supplies, among them a full dozen barrels of flour.

Two men sat at the table, a jug and a couple of tin cups between them. There was the reck of raw liquor in the air. One of the men was lath thin, plainly an emigrant and just as plainly more than half drunk. The other was a short, burly fellow with a broad face, a mop of shaggy, curly black hair, with an anchor tattooed in blue on one bared forearm. He looked at Clay and Jack Casement with a truculent stare, and his voice was rolling and gravelly in his throat.

"Business can wait until tomorrow. I've had a long enough day as it is."

"Not our business," shot back Casement curtly, as he moved past the table and on to the flour barrels.

The burly one shoved back his bench, bounced to his feet, his heavy jaw thrusting in quick anger.

"No," said Clay Roswell. "Stay put."

The burly one swung his head, looked at Clay. He saw the gun at Clay's hip, saw Clay's hand resting casually but definitely close to the butt of the weapon. The thin emigrant shuffled to his feet, weaving a little unsteadily. He, too, Clay admonished with a nod of his head.

"The same, friend. Right as you were."

The thin one sat down again. The burly one demanded: "What's the idea of this? What do you fellers want?"

"A little look around, and then maybe a few questions," Clay told him.

Jack Casement came back to the table. "I want this light for a minute or two."

He took it, went back to the flour barrels again, bent, and looked them over carefully, staring at a mark on one of them and tracing it out with a forefinger. His face was bleak as he brought the light back to the table.

"You," he said to the thin emigrant, "have had about all the liquor you can hold and still keep your feet. Get out of here and sleep it off."

The emigrant stared with sodden eyes, pushed to his feet again, and lurched out into the night. Clay closed the door behind him, turned to watch Casement and the burly one. Casement had both hands spread on the table top and was leaning across it.

"You run this place?" he demanded of the burly one.

"I sure do," was the growling answer. "And I want to know what all this high and mighty . . . ?"

"What's your name?" cut in Casement.

"Not that it's any of your business, but as long as you ask, it's Grimes. Now what . . . ?"

"Where'd you get that flour?" Casement threw each question like a blow.

A gust of anger deepened the whiskey flush in Grimes's broad face. "Hell with you. I don't like your manner and I don't like your tone. Who are you to come bargin' in here so damn' . . . ?"

Clay moved over beside Casement. "Friend," he said, "you can make this just as easy . . . or hard . . . on yourself as you want. We came here to find some answers and we don't leave until we get them. You'll save yourself a lot of trouble if you speak up. You ever hear of a pair of brothers named Pickard?"

Clay was watching the man's eyes closely as he asked this and he clearly saw the startled flicker that leaped up far back in them.

"I see that you do know them," pressed Clay. "I thought you would. Well, they're both dead. I had to kill Jess with this gun. A bunch of teamsters lynched Hoke, but not before he told a lot of things, mainly about murdered teamsters and stolen flour. Now to come back to the main question. Once more . . . where did you get that flour?"

The cold, matter-of-fact manner in which Clay spoke of the violent finish of both the Pickards had its effect. It brought another startled flicker in Grimes's eyes. Waiting for the fellow to answer, Clay tossed a brief question at Casement.

"You found a cross on one of those barrels?"

Casement nodded wearily. "Abbott and Ives flour, and plainly where a cross mark had been scraped off with a knife. Once it was our flour."

Clay's voice went explosively harsh. "All right, Grimes. We know things. We know a lot of things. We want to know more. Lying won't do you a bit of good. The teamsters who lynched Hoke Pickard would be quite happy to give you the same medicine if we tell them you deserve it. So you better speak up. Where'd you get that flour?"

Grimes shrugged, as though recognizing some sort of inevitability. "Bought it. From the Pickards. If they stole it, I didn't know about that."

"So you bought it," purred Clay. "With your own money . . . or with Reed Owen's? Or maybe you didn't buy it at all. Maybe Reed Owen just had it sent out here. He's your boss, ain't he? He owns this place, doesn't he?"

In his way, Grimes was a rough, tough customer. But he wasn't very fast in the head, and this volley of hard-flung questions confused and bewildered him, because the man who asked them seemed to know most of the answers already. The effect of it all held Grimes off balance when, under ordinary conditions, he might have inclined to turn to violent physical action. A thread of bluster crept into his manner.

"I don't know what you're talkin' about," he grumbled.

Jack Casement waved a violent and impatient hand. "Get something straight, once and for all, Grimes. We don't know whether you had an actual hand in the murder of our teamsters and the theft of the flour. But our teamsters will be only too willing to believe you did. And once they get their hands on you with that thought in their mind, they'll give you just what they gave Hoke Pickard. That's no idle threat. It's fact. Now if you want to go back to Fort Churchill and face them, it's all right with me. Roswell, here, and I will take you back, if we don't get the answers we want. You talk straight and you'll be allowed to clear out with a whole hide. Which will it be? Don't try and tell us you don't know what we're talking about. We know better. Let's start again. Do you know Reed Owen?"

Grimes was still for some little time. He had a pretty good berth here. But was it good enough to risk his neck over? How much did he owe to anyone besides himself? He decided he owed nothing.

"All right," he blurted. "I know Reed Owen. And, yeah, he owns this layout. I just work for him. He had that flour delivered out here. I'm tellin' you the truth when I say I didn't know where it came from. I don't know where any of this stuff comes from. All I'm supposed to do is sell it to these jayhawkers along this trail for all I can gouge out of them. That was my job and that's what I been doin'. I ain't stole no flour and I ain't murdered any teamsters. And. . . ."

"That's enough," cut in Casement. "You're free to go, Grimes, and I suggest you go . . . far. Go anywhere, as long as it's well out of this part of the country. It won't be healthy for you if you're seen in these parts again." Casement turned to the door. "Come on, Clay. I've seen and heard enough."

Clay followed him out and over to their horses. Casement stood silently, staring across the desert night. The silence grew long. Then Casement spoke slowly.

"I don't know what to say to you, boy . . . except that I'm sorry. You came to me with a straight story, and I threw the lie in your face. But try and see my side . . . and Katherine's side of this. A man we had worked with from the time the first idea of the big job was born, who we figured a most trustworthy friend . . . and one who demonstrated a lot of valuable ability, is suddenly held up as a thief and a rascal of the lowest order before our very eyes. It was a terrific jolt . . . and perhaps we might be excused for reacting like we did. Try and understand that, will you, Clay?"

Abruptly the iron of resentment that had been in Clay Roswell began to soften. This man beside him was being very humble, and Jack Casement was a big man to be humble in front of anyone. He had been mistaken and now he was admitting it freely and, in his way, asking forgiveness. Clay knew a certain small shame over his own actions. He answered gruffly.

"It's all right, sir. Forget it. I had no right to fly off the handle the way I did."

Casement turned, dropped a hand on Clay's shoulder. "Then it's a fresh start, boy? You're going to stay on with us?"

"I'll stay. Where do we go from here?"

"Why," said Casement, "you're going back to the job. Tell Kitts I'll be along later. Me, I'm going on in to Fort Churchill and face a rascal. I'm going to hold him just as responsible for the deaths of Brad Lincoln and Danny Huggins as you held the Pickards. And I'm going to see that he's punished for it, just as they were punished. His crime is even worse than theirs, for he betrayed as complete a trust as was ever offered a man. He is"—and here Jack Casement's tone broke into harsh explosiveness—"a damned, sly, rotten dog."

"Maybe I better go along with you, sir," suggested Clay. "The man is all you say he is . . . that's been proven. But he could, when faced with the fact, turn dangerous. I think you'd better have me standing at your shoulder."

Casement shook his head. "No. This is between Reed Owen and me. He's my man. I hired him. I trusted him. Now I'll handle him." Casement went into his saddle. "I'll see you at point of wire in a few days, Clay. Get back out there and keep the job rolling."

Clay watched Casement until the night swallowed him. Then he climbed into his own saddle, pointed his horse south and east, and let it pick its own weary jog. The job was calling to him again and the old spark of enthusiasm for it grew within him and fanned bright once more.

Half an hour later, the stocky figure of Grimes came quietly, almost furtively out of the trading post, leaving it dark behind him. He had a rifle in one hand, a pack in the other. In a small canvas sack, slung by a looped cord about his neck and under his shirt, was all the money that the trading post had held. Out back were a couple of horses. If a man rode one of these and put his pack on the other, he'd be set to cover a lot of country.

And out there, far to the north and west, lay the Oregon country. Grimes had never been there, but he'd heard tell about it. Good country, so the word ran, a country where a man could not only lose himself, but where he could do well by himself if he was a shrewd thinker.

Grimes figured he was a shrewd thinker. So, the Oregon country it would be. To hell with this desert. He'd never liked it anyway.

CHAPTER FIFTEEN

Beating out a solitary way back to point of wire, Clay Roswell did not try to hurry. For one thing, there wasn't a shred of hurry left in his horse. During the past several days the buckskin had covered a lot of grueling miles with not too much rest along the way and now it was gaunt and weary and sluggish.

The same numbing weariness lay in its rider, a weariness that was emotional as well as physical. A man could go a long way, mused Roswell, when buoyed up and sustained by the drive of his inner feelings. Like the way it had been when he found Danny Huggins lying dead in the little sand valleys along the main route of the wire.

Anger had been the spur then, a deep, cold, acid anger that fumed and fumed in a man, giving him no rest. And after finding Danny's raided wagon and seeing the ruthless cause of Danny's murder, there had come the driving resolve to run this thing down and bring it to a head, one way or another.

In Churchill, after his talk with the warehouse hand, he'd at last picked up something tangible to go on and this had added an eagerness for the hunt to the anger simmering far back within him. At Bear Wallow Flat the trail had grown hotter, and then had come the shoot-out with the Pickards.

That sort of thing was bound to be one of the peak moments in a man's life. No man could, over the space of a few blazing, savage moments, throw his own life into the balance, match his own gun against that of a dangerous, bitter enemy, kill while facing the strong possibility of being killed, and not expend a great store of emotional stamina. A thing like that, even though a man came out unscathed physically, left him drained and empty and sagging.

Then had come the damning disclosures by Hoke Pickard and the grisly fact of his summary execution by the teamsters. Righteous anger could carry a man through all of these, but could not blot out the inevitable scar that was left.

Still more, there had been that scene at the headquarters wagon. Clay stirred restlessly in his saddle, remembering all the great and small facts of that moment. He had taken another emotional whipping then, when all the fine great spirit and enthusiasm for the job had abruptly gone ash-gray and tasteless to him, when all the drive and effort he'd already given, and that which he'd hoped to continue to give, seemed suddenly meaningless and of no account.

In agreeing to ride out to Myers Wells with Jack Casement, he had done so merely in the stubborn wish to prove his point. He felt that he owed that much to himself, after all he'd done to run down the traitor's trail. Beyond that he'd had no plans, nor felt that he particularly cared, one way or the other.

But now he knew that he did care—that he had cared all along—mightily. For when Casement had turned to him in simple, honest apology and asked him to stay on with the job, Clay's heart had leaped and the beat of his blood grown warm once more.

Yes, a lot of things had happened in the past few days, and, while they had added much, perhaps, they had also taken away. And so he rode under the chill desert stars now, a weary man up on a weary horse.

Somewhere along in the small dead hours of early morning, Clay pulled in, stripped saddle and blanket from his horse, and hunkered down for a period of comfortless rest, thinking more of his horse than of himself. When the first faint thread of gray began to show in the eastern sky, he straightened up stiffly, saddled up again, and went on.

He did not try to go back across the angle of the mountains as he and Jack Casement had come out; instead, he skirted all but the lowest foothills to the south until he struck the main supply route to the point of wire, and there flagged down a lone and early rolling supply wagon. He unsaddled the buckskin again, tied it at lead behind the wagon, lofted his saddle to the top of the load, and climbed up there himself. Here he found a reasonably comfortable spot and went to sleep.

The heat of another day's sun, beating directly down upon him, and the jolting of the wagon under him as it covered a particularly rough stretch awakened him, and he crawled down off the load to a place on the wagon box beside the teamster. A deep drag at the water bag slung to the side of the wagon box helped mightily, cutting the dust, renewing the depleted juices of his body. Normal physical hunger began to gnaw at him and he found partial satisfaction for this by sucking on his pipe.

At midday they came up with a couple of the wire-stringing crew, engaged in fixing a break in the wire.

"Indian work," explained a stocky youngster, strapping on his climbing irons. "Can't figure it as anything else. Damned scoundrels must have throwed a rope over the wire and then just yanked it down. Be a lot of that sort of business to take care of, I guess. Wish the military at Fort Churchill would get off their bottoms and do something about it. I tell you it's no fun stringin' wire with one eye while keeping the other on the look-out for a bunch of prowlin' Goshiutes or White Knives."

He went on, with a boyish grin: "Sure had me a wild dream the other night. Found myself on the top of a pole with forty-'leven wild-eyed war-whoops ganged around the bottom of it. Wasn't enough pole left for me to climb any higher and there sure wasn't any point in tryin' to climb down. I sure was in one hell of a fix. It was real comfortin' to wake up and find it all just a bad dream."

"Isn't this pretty far west for the Indians to be operating?" asked Roswell.

"Not according to all we hear. Understand the Pony Express boys have been having some lively times with the Goshiutes between Churchill and Shell Crossing. That's a neighborhood that ain't too far from here."

It didn't take the youngster and his companion too long to fix the wire break, and then, when they cooked a pot of coffee and fried some bacon beside the trail, Clay and the teamster ate with them. After which, Clay transferred his gear to the light spring wagon the wire boys had, tied the buckskin at lead behind this, and went on with the wire boys, for they would travel much faster than the heavy freighter.

At a little past midafternoon they rolled up to the relay station at Cedar Springs Pass. Here Clay left the buckskin, put his saddle on a fresh horse, and spurred ahead to point of wire. He rode directly to the headquarters wagon. The sun was well down in the west by this time and, in the spread of shade thrown by the wagon, Katherine Casement was listlessly going over some more of the inevitable paperwork.

As Clay pulled to a halt and dismounted, she stood up and faced him, a faint shade of worry in her eyes. Clay anticipated her question.

"Your father has gone back to Fort Churchill for a few days," he said quietly. "Certain items of interest which we found at Myers Wells made him decide on that. He asked me to report this to you."

She nodded, not looking at him. Clay turned to leave, but she stopped him.

"Wait! These . . . these items of interest . . . what were they?"

Clay took his time answering, searching for the right words. He didn't want this girl flaring at him again. "They had to do with the matter I reported to him the other afternoon," Clay said finally.

He saw her flinch a little. Abruptly he was sorry for her. Pretty rough, this sort of life was, for a girl like her. The lone one of her sex out in this crew of rough and toiling men, living out of an oversize spring wagon with all the inevitable discomforts and hardships. All around her a lonely, hostile wilderness. A thick cloud of anxiety and disillusionment hanging over her. She had courage, this girl, and a fine, high pride.

"For any unpleasant moments I've given you, I'm sorry, Kitts," Clay said gravely.

Again he would have turned away and again she stopped him. "Then you've reconsidered? About quitting Dad, I mean?"

Clay felt the flush that ran across his gaunt cheeks. "Yes. Your father and I . . . I think we understand each other completely now."

This told Katherine Casement a great deal. It told her everything, in fact. It certainly told her that there was bitter truth behind Clay Roswell's charges against Reed Owen. It told her that the world could not only be wide and lonely, but also that it could hold a great deal of dismal tragedy in the lives of men and of women. She stared out across that world a little blindly.

And when Clay Roswell turned away a third time, she did not stop him.

CHAPTER SIXTEEN

It was on a gaunt and well used-up horse that Jack Casement rode into Fort Churchill. Except for a couple of short rests, more out of consideration for his horse than for himself, he'd come steadily in from Myers Wells, riding out the night.

It had been a lonely ride and along the solitary miles he'd had plenty of time to think. And in searching the backlog of memory and affairs he had recalled several half-forgotten incidents that, viewed in the light of the stunning disclosures of the past twelve or fifteen hours, took on a brand-new and sinister significance.

He recalled now, how during the initial hurry and fever of preparation for the big job, that several outfits making the long haul of supplies across the Sierras from Sacramento had come to grief. There had been two big double-wagon outfits that had gone off the grade to destruction in the granite depths below the torturous Belden Cañon road.

There had been another outfit that had disappeared completely, loaded wagon, mules, teamster—all of it. There had been minor thefts of food and supplies from wagons all along the line. These things had been reported to him in a more or less fragmentary fashion by Reed Owen who, in a show of high anger, had vowed he was doing all in his power to run down and apprehend the villains responsible.

To Casement, already at Churchill, and working ferociously at the tremendous task of getting all things co-ordinated for the big job ahead, these reports of supply losses and wagon trouble, along with Reed Owen's assurances that future incidents of the sort were being guarded against with all possible alertness, had not assumed too great an importance. They were, as Casement saw them, just some of the inevitable hazards bound to show up in any job as big as the one now occupying all his energy and time. He'd handled other big projects in his time and he knew they always demanded a certain price in loss of both men and material. There was no reason to feel that this job would be an exception. So he had written off the losses and virtually forgotten them.

Until now. And how he wished now that he'd taken time at the moment of happening to investigate those affairs more closely.

Casement left his horse in the care of a hostler at the freight corrals, sought an eating house in town for breakfast, then went directly to his supply warehouse. Here a wagon, newly loaded, was just pulling away from the platform and a warehouseman was going into the office, several papers in his hand. Casement followed him in, to be greeted heartily.

"Mister Casement. This is a surprise. Glad to see you. How are things on the job?"

"Moving along, Lafe," said Casement. "Reed Owen around?"

Lafe Hubbard, the warehouseman, shook his head. "He was here most of yesterday, but he pulled out late in the afternoon. Didn't say where he was going, but he did say he'd probably get back sometime today. Anything I can help you with?"

Casement was silent for a moment, then nodded. "Have a chair, Lafe." Casement rummaged through the desk drawers, came up with a couple of stale Virginia cheroots, handed one over to Lafe Hubbard, lit up the other himself. Casement leaned back a little wearily, fixed Hubbard with a grave glance.

"You've been with me quite a while, haven't you, Lafe?"

135

Hubbard nodded quickly. "Right from the start, Mister Casement. Came across the Sierras with the first bunch of wagons and helped build this very warehouse. Figgered first I might skin a wagon outfit for you, but bein' here when the first supplies started comin' in, I just sort of fell into this job. I ain't kickin'. It's been a good job, all things considered."

"And you've done your part of it well, Lafe," said Casement quietly. "Now I'm going to ask you to scratch your memory and think back quite a ways. Do you remember some of the supply outfits we lost, making the long drag across the Sierras?"

"Sure do," asserted Hubbard. "I remember one outfit, lead wagon and back action, a big Merivale outfit, that just disappeared complete, somewhere between Granite Ford and Yankee Peak. I remember that one particular, because it just didn't make sense to me that a big rig like that one should just vanish into thin air like a puff of dust. Being more or less familiar with that stretch of country . . . I did a little placer minin' there before taking on with you . . . I asked Reed Owen permission to head back there and look around and see what I could find. He wouldn't let me go, though, sayin' I was needed here and that he'd look into the matter himself. Don't know whether he ever did or not. Anyhow, I never heard anything more about it."

A shadowed gleam showed in Jack Casement's eyes. "You recall anything else of the sort, Lafe?"

"Well, there were a couple of outfits that went off the Belden Cañon grade, as I remember."

"That's right, there were." Casement nodded. "Now there is a big point, Lafe. Have you any idea what it was those wagons were hauling in the way of supplies?"

"Yes, sir," said Hubbard. "Mostly they were haulin' grub supplies, flour and bacon and salt and coffee and such. Some tools, too, and clothes. Reason I know is that those were the things we needed most at the time, to take care of the men who were doin' all the building we had to have . . . bunkhouses, corrals, finishin' up this warehouse . . . things like that. Our other stuff, wire, insulators, everything like that, all came in later. I remember Reed Owen saying how lucky we were that it was just grub supplies we'd lost, for that could be replaced a lot more easy than wire and instruments and other gear that couldn't."

"Yes," said Casement, his tone wearily dry, "I can understand him saying that, now."

Something in the way Jack Casement said these words caused his warehouseman to swing his head and stare. "Something wrong, Mister Casement?"

"Yes, Lafe, very much so. Now you've been working with our supplies long enough to know the ropes. All the main organizational work is done, the system set up. From now on, handling our supplies is pretty much routine. We send orders for the stuff we want to the main office in Sacramento. They send the stuff in across the mountains and we check it in at this end, then send it as it is needed out to the job at wire's end. That's about the picture, isn't it?"

"That's it, Mister Casement," said Hubbard, wondering.

"Suppose," said Casement slowly, "I made you supply boss. Think you could handle it?"

"Me!" ejaculated Hubbard. "You mean . . . me? Supply boss? What about Reed Owen? What . . . ?"

"Reed Owen," said Casement grimly, "is no longer a member of our organization, Lafe. And as of this moment, if you'll take it . . . and I hope you will . . . Reed Owen's job is yours. How about it?"

It took a little time for Lafe Hubbard to get over his amazement. Then he steadied and his glance was very direct. "If you want me to . . . I'll take it. And thanks. I think I can do a job for you, Mister Casement."

"I know you can, Lafe. And of one thing I'm very sure. I can trust you. That's the most important angle of all."

Outside, a wagon came creaking up and a teamster's yell echoed. "Hey, Lafe . . . Lafe Hubbard! How about gettin' me loaded up? I got a long way to go."

Hubbard got to his feet and moved to the office door. Casement held him for just a moment more.

"Keep this to yourself for a while, Lafe. Let me make the announcement to the other men. And when Reed Owen shows up, tell him I want to see him."

"Just as you say, Mister Casement." Hubbard nodded. Then he went on out.

For a long couple of hours, Jack Casement sat there in the warehouse office, brooding over this thing. The more he thought about it, the more damning the evidence grew. Even his talk with Lafe Hubbard had added to the inevitable conviction.

The day wore along. At first, during the long ride in from Myers Wells, Casement had known a certain reluctance over the prospect of facing Reed Owen and laying the cards on the table. It wasn't a pleasant thing to consider, this necessity of meeting a man who had been considered a long-time friend and confidant and co-worker and then stripping aside the false armor of the man and exposing the calculated villainy that lay underneath. Nor could the matter go that far and no further. For Reed Owen was as surely responsible for the deaths of Brad Lincoln and Danny Huggins as were Jess and Hoke Pickard and deserved just as grim and final punishment. This, also, must be seen to. Baldly exposing Owen meant signing his death warrant, once the word got out among the teamsters.

All these things had Jack Casement considered and there was the heavy grind of bitterness in him because of them. Yet, as he waited now for the man to show up, he knew, along with the bitterness, a grim and chilling resolve to see the matter through to the final dreary end, regardless.

It was well along in the day when Casement heard the small echo of voices outside, then quick, sharp steps, and there was Reed Owen, standing in the office doorway. Owen exclaimed with heartiness—a too-effusive heartiness, so it seemed to Casement.

"Jack! This is a surprise. Nothing wrong out at end of wire, is there? Supplies reaching there steadily, aren't they?"

"Not all, but enough, perhaps," was Casement's grim reply.

"Know what you mean," said Reed Owen, dropping into a chair. "That Danny Huggins affair. Dirty business. Those Pickards . . . what miserable scoundrels they turned out to be. Boys down at the corrals were telling me about them, and about their finish. Damned good riddance, if you ask me."

"Wasn't it?" Casement nodded dryly. "How did you first come to meet those fellows?"

"Just one of those things," said Owen easily. "Somebody pointed me out to them one day in town and told them I was connected with the company. They came over, introduced themselves, and asked for wagon jobs. We needed men at the time and they looked all right to me. So I put them to work hauling poles down out of the mountains. They showed up as the best two men we had on the job, so, when you told me you were on the look for somebody to take charge of all our wagons, I recommended them to you. I was wrong there, of course. I was sure taken in by them. You've heard about their finish, I suppose?"

"I've heard. That's why I'm here. Clay Roswell did a mighty fine job, running down those damned whelps."

"Now didn't he," agreed Reed Owen. "Guess I owe Roswell an apology. He's turned out to be a damned good wagon boss." He said this lightly, almost carelessly, then added: "Of course I don't go for this idea of one man taking it on himself to have another man lynched . . . not even a damned thief like Hoke Pickard turned out to be. A thing of that sort should be left up to properly constituted authority. I've heard considerable talk in town about that affair and there's a lot of people who don't like it a bit."

"Clay Roswell," said Jack Casement steadily, "didn't lynch Hoke Pickard . . . or order him lynched. A bunch of our teamsters who had known Brad Lincoln and Danny Huggins and called them friend did the lynching on their own. What Clay Roswell did was to make a deal with Hoke Pickard, saying he'd get the best break he could for Pickard with the proper authorities, providing Pickard would open up and talk. You see, Clay figured, and smartly so, that there was somebody else in the dirty business besides the Pickards, and he wanted to get the deadwood on them, too. So he made that offer to Hoke Pickard, then did his best to carry out his part of the bargain. He wasn't even close around when the teamsters took matters into their own hands and strung Hoke Pickard up."

Jack Casement was watching Reed Owen closely as he spoke and he saw that long jaw of Owen's tighten perceptibly, while a certain veiled blankness masked the black restlessness of his eyes. Reed Owen's chair creaked slightly as he stirred.

"Wouldn't take too much stock in anything Hoke Pickard said under such circumstances. That's like holding a gun to a man's head and telling him to say something. In which case a fellow like Hoke Pickard would say anything or tell any amount and kind of damn' lies in an effort to save his neck. Isn't that what a court of law would call obtaining information or evidence under duress? I think so."

"Perhaps," agreed Casement, the grimness in his tone unconsciously deepening. "Yet it was a case of working with the best weapons at hand and I say that Clay Roswell was justified. And I don't think Hoke Pickard lied."

Reed Owen got out of his chair, took a short turn up and down the office. Jack Casement's blue eyes followed the man, reflecting a growing bleakness.

"Then Hoke Pickard did do some talking?" asked Owen.

"He did . . . plenty. And some of the things he told are awful hard to believe. At least, they were at first. But now, in the light of different things that I recall taking place in the past . . . along with other developments . . . they become less hard to believe. As Clay Roswell said when he told me the story, it makes sense. It points a finger."

Reed Owen, taking another turn around the office, stopped at a window and stood staring out of it. "Who else was present besides Roswell, when Hoke Pickard did this talking?"

"No one. The deal was strictly between Clay and Pickard." Casement, still watching closely, saw the tension in Owen's face break slightly.

"Just what did Hoke Pickard tell Roswell?" demanded Owen.

"A number of things," Casement said. "But before we go into that, I want to consider again several things I've been remembering, certain incidents that took place 'way back when we first began setting up headquarters here at Churchill. We were busy then, mighty busy, getting everything organized and set up for the big job. We had a lot of wagons moving across the mountains from Sacramento, hauling in supplies. Not all of those wagons that started from Sacramento arrived here. As I recall, there was one big double-wagon outfit, along with driver, mules, and everything, that just seemed to vanish into thin air. There were a couple of other outfits that went off the Belden Cañon grade."

Casement paused, tapping restless fingers on the desk top. It was as though he were fixing all these incidents clearly in his mind's eye once more. But it was really a deliberate pause, to pile up the effect. Presently he went on.

"At the time, when this word came to me, I didn't pay it too much attention, figuring they were operational losses to be expected in rough country. Besides, I had plenty else on my mind. Now I wish I'd have found time to investigate those incidents a little more closely. That might have headed off later troubles. Anyhow, on checking back now, I find that those lost outfits all were loaded with food supplies for the most part. Just like the wagons we've had looted since starting the big job. And that strikes me as being more than coincidence. Don't you think so, Reed?"

Owen kept staring out the window. "Hadn't given it too much thought," he answered harshly. "It's your picture you're building. You're driving at something. What is it?"

"The truth. Reed, you asked me what it was that Hoke Pickard told Clay Roswell. Well, here's part of it . . . the big part. He admitted that he and his brother Jess managed those two steals that cost Brad Lincoln and Danny Huggins their lives, and the company two wagonloads of flour. He admitted using three transient bums to drive the light wagons the stolen flour was loaded into. But mainly he admitted that there was one big boss directing the whole dirty business. And that boss was . . . you."

Now Reed Owen came around, that strange, masked blackness about his face and behind the deep-seated glitter in his black eyes. "Me! And you believe that?"

Jack Casement met and held the look. "Well . . . ?"

Words broke from Reed Owen in a torrent. "So that's what all this mealy-mouthed yapping leads up to, eh? Casement, I always gave you credit for being a real smart man. Yet you can't see through this. You're letting yourself be taken in like a bald-faced kid. But not me. That fellow Roswell will have to think faster than that to pin any such damn' fool charge on me." He moved over to the desk, pounded a fist on it. "Roswell's cooked up one fine little picture for you. Now I'll draw you another.

While you're recalling things, recall this. That first day you saw Roswell . . . when he came into the Shoshone Bar and tore into Jess and Hoke Pickard. He was out to kill both of them, if he'd been allowed to. Later, in your own cabin, he gave you his story of why he had it in for the Pickards. Maybe he was telling the truth about that. In light of what the Pickards turned out to be, he probably was. Now let's look what happened."

Reed Owen moved up and down the room once more, then swung again to face Casement.

"All right. So Roswell ran down the trail of our stolen wagons, and that trail led him to the Pickards. He shot and killed Jess Pickard. He cripples up Hoke Pickard, brings him back to Churchill. And here he very conveniently manages to get Hoke lynched by a bunch of teamsters. All of which effectively closes the mouths of both Jess and Hoke Pickard, so nobody else can ask them any questions and find out any answers. But Roswell claims that Hoke Pickard told him things, things that you're using to make a damn' fool charge against me, Jack. I thought you had better sense than that. Here's why." Owen banged a fist on the desk again. "You admit that nobody else but Roswell heard what Hoke Pickard had to say. So, for all you know for certain, Hoke might not have said anything. How do you know how far Roswell is lying? Particularly about me. For some reason, Roswell has hated my guts, right from the start. Just why, I don't know. But he has. All right. He got even with the Pickards. And how better to take a swing at me than by coming to you with a wild cock-and-bull story, saying that Hoke Pickard told him this and that? Where's his proof? Let him produce somebody else who heard what Hoke Pickard had to say. He can't. He took damn' good care of that. Yeah, Jack, I thought you were a bigger man than this . . . and a smarter one."

Jack Casement had sat absolutely still throughout Reed Owen's outburst. And he thought to himself that this man was clever and that he'd worked out a logical premise that might have been convincing, placing his word against that of Clay Roswell's. Yes, it might have been convincing, except for other things. One of these was that Owen had reacted to the initial accusation a little too quickly and vehemently. An innocent man would have been more stunned and incredulous. Besides all those other angles. Casement cleared his throat harshly and spoke of them.

"That wasn't all that Hoke Pickard had to say. For instance, he said that you'd gone into the trading business on quite a scale, Owen. That you were the real owner of the trading posts at Myers Wells and Bear Wallow and Sugar Pine. There might be others, but Hoke Pickard was sure of these three. So, you own them or you don't. Which is it?"

This was a solid body blow. Reed Owen hesitated a little too long before blurting: "Another lie! Why in hell would I be wanting to own any trading post, let alone a string of them?"

"Because that would be a mighty handy way to get rid of supplies stolen from us, while making a hell of a profit," rapped Casement. "Let me tell you something. Last night Clay Roswell and I rode out to Myers Wells. A fellow named Grimes was in charge. At first he was a little stubborn. But when I identified some barreled flour he had on hand as flour stolen from our wagons, he decided he'd be a fool to take the blame. He told us that you, Reed Owen, were his boss. That you owned the place. Now don't try and tell me I'm making that up. I was there, and I know what I saw and what I heard."

Now the cold anger that had been building and seething in him over the past hours blazed up in Jack Casement. It was his turn to lean forward and pound a fist on the desk.

"You can't slide out of this, Owen. That outfit of ours that disappeared, coming across the Sierras . . . you know damn' well where it went. Those wagons that went off the grade into the depths of Belden Cañon . . . I'll stake my life they weren't loaded when they went over. No, they'd been looted and then driven over. If I'd taken the trouble to ride up there and find a way to the bottom of that cañon, I know what I'd have found. Dead mules and smashed-up wagons . . . but none of the flour and other supplies they'd once been loaded with. That had all been taken care of beforehand, hadn't it? You'd seen to that. You'd seen that it was spread around in your trading posts to be sold to some poor devil emigrants at robber prices. The drivers of those outfits? Bought off or dead at the bottom of Belden Cañon along with their mules and smashed-up wagons."

The fury in Casement lifted him to his feet. Reed Owen stared at him as though from behind some invisible wall. Suddenly there was a heavy, brutal, venal cast to Reed Owen's face. But he still tried to brazen it out.

"Lies," he said in flat, dull tones. "Damned lies. Crazy pipe dreams. And no real proof. . . ."

"Lies be damned!" growled Casement. "Proof! I got all the proof I need. Owen, you're a thief, a traitor, and a black, dirty murderer. And to think that once I accepted you as a fine friend and a man I could depend on with my life. That was the biggest mistake in judgment I ever made in my life. You're exactly the same breed as the men you tried your damnedest to foist on me as wagon bosses . . . Jess and Hoke Pickard. You deserve just what Hoke Pickard got, and I'm going to see that you get it. By God, I am."

Reed Owen's lips writhed, showing his teeth. "That's what you think, Casement. Different . . . here!"

Jack Casement, realizing suddenly what Owen was about, tried to throw himself around the desk at the man. But before he could get there, Reed Owen had cleared a stubby Derringer from a pocket and he threw the slug into Casement at this short, pointblank range.

Under the smash of the heavy slug Casement lurched, spun, balanced back against the desk for a moment, then slid slowly, almost gently down.

Moving very fast, Reed Owen went out the office door, jumped off the end of the platform, and was gone around the far corner of the warehouse before Lafe Hubbard, the warehouseman, investigating that muffled shot, found Jack Casement lying in his own blood.

CHAPTER SEVENTEEN

Out at point of wire, they went down that twisting, sage-guarded valley toward the east, tightening their belts and girding themselves for the assault on the rugged bleakness of the sun-scorched mountains that lay ahead. The wilderness was throwing all its weapons against them now. Of these, one of the most potent was the first people of this wilderness—the Indians.

The Goshiutes were growing steadily bolder. Wagon men carried ready weapons on the seats beside them. Weapons were stacked with the tools of the digging crews and no man of the wire-stringing crew went up a pole without a companion on guard beneath him. Up front, remembering what had happened to two of their number, the survey gang moved with especial caution. Clay Roswell, on the move up and down the busy scene, rode always with his revolver at his hip and a rifle in the scabbard under his stirrup leather. And the poles marched on and the gleaming wire spread its graceful swoops to the wind.

The relay station at Cedar Springs Pass had been completed and instruments set up. Now, across the miles between the pass and Fort Churchill, the magic of the telegraph was beginning to carry from tapping key to tapping key. Tests were run, then more tests. Men of the crews, when some sort of chore brought them to the pass, listened to the key, marveled at the magic of it, then went back to their toil with renewed fervor. For here was proof and meaning of their labor. This was the answer to the big job. This made all the toil and sweat and hardship and danger worthwhile.

Clay Roswell, after delivering her father's message to Katherine Casement, did not speak to her again. He saw her nearly every time he had cause to pass by the headquarters wagon, but had no excuse to stop and doubted that he would have been welcome in any event. She was grave and unsmiling and pre-occupied and seemed intent only on keeping up the records and other paperwork that her father had entrusted with her.

Tom Hughes, the boss surveyor, spent some time with her, bringing in the data supplied by his gang, and advising her on this, but most of the time she was alone, and, as she seemed to wish it so, the men respected that wish.

There were times when she would just sit and stare at the lonely sage slopes, but Clay knew she was not seeing them. She was seeing something else, the tragedy of a betrayed friendship. Clay did not feel any better, knowing that he was the prime cause in uncovering that betrayal, yet common sense told him it was better brought to light now than later. He doubted, though, that she'd ever thank him for it.

Clay had given the word of Reed Owen's perfidy to only one other person besides Jack and Katherine Casement. He told Bill Yerkes about it. The grizzled teamster listened in silence, then swore softly but at length. Then he thought it over for a moment.

"You know, lad . . . now that you've told me, it somehow don't surprise me too much. There was something about that feller I never could quite put a finger on. Now I know what it was. He was slickery. There was a shiftiness in him, a certain bluster. His eyes were too close together and they never would quite look square at you. But the gol-blasted dirty gall of him. Stealin' from the company that paid him, double-crossin' Jack Casement, and all the rest of us for that matter. And by God, he's just as much responsible for the deaths of Danny Huggins and Brad Lincoln as them cussed Pickards were. Puttin' it straight up and down, he's a damned murderer as well as a slimy thief."

To which Clay nodded. "All of that, Bill. And I'm just a little uneasy as to what he might do when Jack Casement throws those charges in his teeth."

Bill Yerkes grunted and spat. "Hah. Don't you worry about that. Jack Casement ain't the biggest man in the world measured physical, but he's a chunk of dynamite in more ways than one. He'll take care of Mister Reed Owen and he'll do it right."

It was after dark. They'd had supper and were sitting by a campfire, smoking and easing away the fatigue of the day. Then it was Clay who heard the rataplan of speeding hoofs first, and, as he cocked his head to listen, Bill Yerkes picked up the sound.

"Now there's somebody in a hell of a hurry," remarked the old teamster. "Wonder what's liftin' him along so fast?"

Clay got to his feet, faced the sound. The pound of hoofs swelled louder and a rider burst out of the darkness, setting up his mount in a sliding halt. Clay recognized the fellow as a roustabout and helper from the Cedar Springs Pass station.

"What is it?" rapped Clay. "Something wrong? Indian trouble maybe?"

The roustabout shook his head. "Miss Casement . . . where'll I find her?"

"What do you want her for?"

"Casement"—gulped the fellow—"Jack Casement, her father. Message just came in over the wire from Fort Churchill. Some kind of ruckus at Churchill, I guess. Anyhow, that Reed Owen feller shot Jack Casement."

The roustabout would have whirled away, spurred on. But Clay grabbed him by the arm, pulled him out of the saddle.

"Take it slow! You're sure of what you're saying? There's no mistake? You mean . . . Jack Casement is dead?"

"No, not dead. But bad hurt. And all I know is what the key operator at the pass told me. He said to get the word to Miss Casement as fast as I could. That's what I'm tryin' to do. You had no call to yank me off my horse. Now . . . where'll I find that girl?"

"Never mind about that," rapped Clay. "I'll take the word to her myself."

Clay headed off through the night at a run. A cold, gray emptiness seemed to rise up in him and choke him. Grisly dread rode on his shoulder.

The headquarters wagon was a couple of hundred yards distant. There was a small campfire burning beside it. Katherine Casement and quiet, steady Tom Hughes sat beside it. They both looked up as Clay came into the circle of firelight. The girl, marking the look on Clay's face, came to her feet, and her words rang sharp with quick anxiety.

"There's something wrong?"

Clay moved slowly around the fire, towered close above her. It had to be said, so he said it simply.

"Get hold of yourself, Kitts. Your father has been hurt. The message has just come through from Fort Churchill."

She swayed and Clay put out a steadying arm. "Hurt . . . Dad hurt?" she whispered brokenly. "How . . . ?"

Something more had to be said, even worse than before. "Reed Owen shot him. Your father's not dead, but of course you've got to get to Churchill as quickly as possible." Clay looked past her at Tom Hughes. "Tom, I'll want that light buckboard of yours and your best team. See about getting them ready, will you? I'll take Kitts in myself."

Tom Hughes knew the ways of a wild frontier and, though the news shocked him, he wasted no time in argument. He asked only one question. "Reed Owen shot Jack Casement. Why . . . in God's name . . . why?"

"Talk to Bill Yerkes later, Tom. He'll give you an idea. Now, get that buckboard!"

Hughes rushed away. Clay looked down at the girl. Her face was dead white and her eyes squeezed tightly shut. But not tightly enough to keep the tears from squeezing through and running down her cheeks. Her lips and chin were trembling.

"I knew it," she cried softly, her voice a thin little wail. "I knew something . . . would happen . . . like this. All day I've felt it . . . something inside . . . told me. Oh, Dad . . . Dad."

Then the flood broke and she sobbed brokenly. Clay's arm went clear around her shaking shoulders and she did not pull away. She just leaned against his chest and wept.

He gave her a little time, then shook her gently. "You'll have to get a few things together, Kitts. Hughes will be here any minute with that buckboard."

Bill Yerkes came up out of the night. "Anything I can do, Clay?"

"Yeah. Get a water bag, some grub, and my rifle. There's extra ammunition in my saddlebags. I'm taking Miss Casement to Fort Churchill in Tom Hughes's buckboard. We'll be ready to leave in a couple of minutes, Bill."

Yerkes hurried off into the night again. Katherine Casement had quieted a little. Clay gave her a pat on the shoulder. "Stout feller. That's better. Now go get your gear."

She nodded mechanically, turned, and climbed into the headquarters wagon where she slept. She was soon back, holding a coat and a small gripsack. Clay helped her into her coat; she was like a stunned child. Tom Hughes brought the buckboard whirling up, got down, and handed the reins to Clay.

"You'll take over the job, Tom," said Clay.

Hughes nodded. "We'll keep going."

He helped the girl into the rig, put her gripsack at her feet. Bill Yerkes came up, panting, carrying what Clay had asked for.

151

These things were stowed and Clay said: "The wagons are your chore, Bill. May be some time before I get back. For I'll be taking a trail, probably. And it may be a long one. I intend to stick to it until I get results."

Bill Yerkes knew what he meant and murmured in reply: "The best wishes of all of us will be ridin' with you while you run that whelp down, boy. When you face him, he deserves nothing. Remember that. Good luck."

Clay settled himself beside the girl, kicked off the brake. The buckboard team surged into their collars. The night opened and took the buckboard in.

Bill Yerkes and Tom Hughes stood, staring after it. When the sound of it had died away, Hughes turned to the old teamster. "I'm still trying to figure . . . why? Roswell said you could tell me, Bill."

Bill explained as best he could, telling what he knew. "Jack Casement must have cornered Owen, so Owen shot him," he ended. "It's a dirty trail, Tom . . . from start to finish. And it sure makes you wonder about men."

The buckboard team was fresh, but, after letting the animals get rid of their first burst of spirit, Clay Roswell held them down to a pace calculated to get the best out of them without wearing them out in the first half of the journey. For it was a long drag into Churchill.

Katherine Casement sat wordlessly beside Clay, her worry and grief locked deeply within her. The first savage shock was wearing off. Clay respected her silence, knowing that this was kinder than any talk of comfort. Besides, he had his own thoughts, and out of these a cold resolve was forming. He'd have to wait until they got to Fort Churchill, to get all the details. For all he knew, this thing had been a showdown gunfight between Jack Casement and Owen. Maybe Casement had got lead into Owen—maybe he'd killed him. Which would have been the perfect answer.

But if Reed Owen had come out of it unscathed, then there would be a trail to take and follow, the trail Clay had spoken of to Bill Yerkes. And no matter how far that trail, or where it led, Clay promised himself grimly that he'd run it down and exact final payment. That was his resolve.

They sped on along the far length of the sage valley, their road paralleling the line of marching poles, which, as they whisked past, were splinters of dark substance against the stars. In time, light winked ahead at the crest of a slope, and, when the buckboard topped this, the squat bulk of the Cedar Springs Pass relay station was before them. Here Clay pulled to a stop, jumped down, and went in. Two men were there and they looked at Clay questioningly.

"Miss Casement is outside," he explained curtly. "I'm taking her to her father. A cup of coffee would do her good. And is there any further word about Jack Casement?"

There was a stove and a pot of coffee steaming on it. One of the men poured a cup, carried it onside. The telegraph operator, fussing about his telegrapher's key, said: "Another message came in, not five minutes ago. The news is better. Casement was badly wounded, all right. But it seems the military doctor they brought in from the post at Churchill feels pretty confident. And there was another message you could be interested in. A westbound Pony Express rider had a rough go of it, fighting off a bunch of Goshiutes that tried to lay an ambush right at the edge of the desert. Which means the damned savages could be on the prowl anywhere between here and Churchill. The military is sending out a patrol to try and locate them. So you'd be smart not to take anything for granted on the rest of your drive in."

"Damn the Goshiutes," rapped Clay. "It's that fellow Reed Owen I'm interested in. Any word about him? Have they got him rounded up at Churchill, or did he get away?"

"Don't know," answered the operator. "Never had any word about Reed Owen, except that he was the one who shot Casement. If you can spare a couple of minutes, I'll try and find out something."

Clay waited, moving restlessly up and down. The operator began tapping out a call, got acknowledgment, then clattered out a swift message. He threw a switch and the answer came back, the operator reading alertly what was just a meaningless mechanical clatter to Clay.

"Reed Owen's disappeared. A bunch of teamsters are combing every corner of Churchill for him, but nothing has turned up so far. That damned, crooked, slippery son-of-a-bitch!" The operator closed his relay switch with more force than necessary.

Clay went out, got into the buckboard again. That cup of hot coffee had helped Katherine Casement. She was sitting up a little straighter.

"The news is better," Clay told her. "They got a military doctor for your father and he feels quite confident."

He heard the deep, shaking breath of relief that she drew. Then her voice, small and muffled: "Thank you. You are being . . . very kind."

The western run of the Cedar Springs Pass was for several miles between gaunt rock rims that lifted, black and craggy, on either hand. In places the road ran directly over sheets of cap rock, in others was a deep-rutted way blanketed with dust, cut and powdered by the ponderous wheels of the pole wagons and other weighty freighters. Over the rocky places the speeding buckboard set up a clatter and a rattle, but in the deep dust it churned along almost noiselessly, the hoofs of the team beating up a muffled echo. Dust lifted, invisible in the dark, but the smell of it was there, and the taste of it, sun-scorched and bitter.

Clay knew every turn and twist, every level and every down pitch of this road, for he'd been over it so many times. He drove by reflex, his thoughts far out ahead. At times the jounce and sway of the buckboard brought the pressure of Katherine Casement's shoulder against his and the contact awakened a strange protectiveness in him. If he'd known any shade of resentment toward this girl for the scathing anger she had shown him when he'd first brought the word of Reed Owen's villainy to her and her father, there was none left now. Instead, he knew only gentleness and the wish to comfort her.

The best way to do this, he knew, was to keep his silence and to get her to Churchill as quickly as possible. That news they'd had at Cedar Springs Pass helped mightily. He could sense that the tension in the girl had lessened.

Nor was Clay forgetting the final warning of the operator at Cedar Springs Pass. If the Goshiutes were on the prowl this far west, it behooved any man to take nothing for granted. The Pony Express route was not too far north of this spot and a few miles of country was nothing for the Goshiutes to cover. So, as he rolled the buckboard along, Clay maintained a steadily searching alertness.

The Goshiutes, he knew, were not of the superb warrior breed like the tribes of the Great Plains. They were much further down the human scale than the Sioux or the Blackfeet or the Arapahoes. They did not have the fire and dash and the high, bright pride and intelligence of these. The Goshiutes were creatures of the sagebrush coverts, slinking and treacherous. They were arrant cowards in open fight, but given the odds and the cover to work in they were as merciless and deadly dangerous as a coiled rattlesnake.

The miles rolled steadily under them and the road broke from the rocky jaws of the pass and pitched into the first open, far-running slope beyond. Here the dark seemed to thin and the stars drop closer. Ahead and far below lay the shadowed gulf that was the desert, at the far edge of which lay Fort Churchill. Clay set the team to a faster pace, riding the brake just enough to keep the buckboard from climbing up on the broncos' haunches.

He had taken another survey of what he could make of the night and it was a still and empty world, seemingly. So he settled back on the seat, feeling that the trail was clear. And that was when he heard the flutter and thud as an arrow struck home.

The off bronco of the team reared, lunged, kicked, and went abruptly crazy. It surged off the road, despite all Clay could do with the reins, dragging its companion in harness with it. The buckboard skidded sideways, humped wildly over an upthrust spine of rock, almost turned over. Clay sawed savagely at the reins, fighting the crazed, arrow-stung horse. At the same time he rapped a harsh order at the girl beside him.

"Hang on! And get as low as you can!"

Somehow, and he didn't quite know how, he fought the team back onto the road, with the buckboard still upright. But even through the wild urgency of the moment he heard the impact of more arrows striking, and he knew that he had in front of him a pair of mortally wounded animals that might go down in their tracks without warning and at any moment. Yet, while the animals were still on their feet, he would make what use he could of them. He brought the whip into play, yelling harshly at the animals.

This, he thought savagely, was the animal cunning of the Goshiutes. Get the horses first, the bigger and easier-to-hit target. Get them, and then the occupants of the rig would be easy. That was the way the Goshiutes would figure it.

Under the biting agony of the arrows in them and the flailing whip, the team tore on down the road at a laboring gallop, the buckboard bouncing and careening behind them. They were past the immediate danger spot, but Clay Roswell knew it was an advantage that couldn't last very long. Even as he thought of this the off bronco began to slow, stiff-legged now, humping up. To the girl Clay said: "Get ready to leave this thing!"

That off bronco came to a complete halt, then went to its knees, flopped over on its side, kicking spasmodically. The buckboard slewed around, tilted. Clay was out of it instantly, pulling the girl after him. He paused only to grab his rifle and his saddlebags.

"Stick close! Right at my heels!"

As they dodged past the team, the other bronco collapsed in its tracks. Then Clay was racing down the empty road ahead, Katherine Casement speeding beside him. The road dipped, crossing a shallow gulch that angled a descending way along the mountain flank. Clay left the road here, following the twisting wind of the gulch along its dark depths.

It was rough going, but they kept at it. The gulch broke sharply to the left, deepening between high-reared banks, and here the dark was complete. Clay came to a halt, low-crouched, and the girl dropped beside him.

Clay tore at the flap buckles of his saddlebags, got them open, shoveled a couple of double handfuls of cartridges for the Henry rifle into his pockets. Then he went still, listening. He could hear the soft, quick, panting breath of his companion and the quickening surge of his own blood thundered in his ears. But he could tell that they had won a temporary break. Yet, only temporary. The Goshiutes would soon be sniffing out their trail, like slinking night animals. Clay dropped a hand on the girl's arm.

"You're not hurt? None of those damned arrows . . . ?"

He could feel a strand of her hair brush his face as she shook her head. "No," she murmured. "No. I'm all right. I can go on."

She had courage, Kitts Casement had. With enough on her

mind to go completely to pieces, she showed no sign of faltering. But Clay knew there was no point in trying to comfort her with false hopes, so he didn't try.

"We got a tough night ahead, Kitts," he told her softly. "But if we play it smart, we got a chance. Give me the best you've got. Come on."

They went on down the gulch for another considerable distance, leaving the saddlebags behind. This freed one of Clay's hands to give the girl aid over the rougher places. But progress was slow, here in these black depths, and Clay knew they had to do better than this. They had to get back to a ridge top, where the going would be better and where the light of the stars would help.

They climbed the slope to their right, topped the ridge there. Clay paused to listen and look, then went on again, setting a driving pace. The ridge slanted down, ever down, taking them toward the desert. Clay set a relentless pace. It was the only choice, their lone chance for safety. To put distance and more distance between them and the pursuit he knew was sniffing relentlessly after them.

Clay's thoughts reached backward. There was no way he could have avoided the surprise attack. The buckboard had to stick to the road and a man's senses, no matter how alert, could only reach so far and no farther into the shrouding cover of the night. Lying in wait along the road, the Goshiutes had had all the advantage. The big break of luck for Clay and Kitts Casement was that neither of them had been struck by that first volley of arrows and that the buckboard team had not been dropped on the spot. The final short dash down the road before the stricken animals had gone down had given them this long chance for their lives.

Had he been alone, Clay would not have been too disturbed over the set-up, fairly certain that he could outpace and outwit the Indians. But he had Kitts along, and that made all the difference. This could turn out to be a very brutal night for her. Courage she had a world of, but there was a limit to her strength, and these wilderness miles were long.

Clay did not let up on his driving pace until he knew, by her increased stumbling, that Kitts had to have rest. So, in a pocket of blackness just under the ridge crest, he called a halt. Kitts dropped beside him, and, when he reached out a hand to touch her shoulder, he could tell by her trembling that exhaustion was beginning to exact its inevitable drag on her strength.

"Good girl," he told her. "Great girl. Your father would be proud of you."

She did not answer, just huddled there, her breath sobbing in and out. Every instinct in Clay shouted at him to be up and gone again, for he knew that pursuit was coming and that it was pushing close. He could see no sign of it, could hear no sign of it, but he knew it was there. He could tell by the instinctive bristling of the hair along the nape of his neck.

The Goshiutes weren't far away. This was their country, had been through the ages. Low down the scale as they were, they owned all the instinct and cunning for the chase that an animal might have. There was no limit to their blood lust, or their cruelty. They could trail through the dark as easily as a white man could by day. It was an animal acuteness in them that made them so dangerous.

Kitts's breathing began to soften and she stirred. "I'm rested," she murmured. "I can go on . . . now."

She started to straighten up, but Clay dragged her flat with a sweep of his hand. For, breaking out of the dim woof of the night with spectral suddenness and moving down the ridge top at a shuffling trot, a squat and wild shape was limned against the stars.

Clay thought the Goshiute would pass them by, but when

almost directly above them the figure stopped, and it seemed to Clay that by the swing of the shaggy head, the Goshiute brave was staring right down at them. One thing was certain. By some wild instinct the brave sensed their presence.

An unearthly, gobbling yelp echoed across the mountain still-ness, a sound more blood chilling than the cry of any animal could have been. Then the brave was whirling toward cover. The bullet from Clay's rifle caught him halfway through the move and the brave went down in a tumbling heap, dying hard with a mewing, choking, scrabbling sound. Clay pulled Kitts to her feet and once more they were fleeing down the ridge.

No chance of laying a tangled trail now. That gobbling yelp and the flat crash of the rifle shot would bring racing pursuit now.

How long and far they ran, Clay had no idea. But even his tempered muscles were feeling the strain when Kitts Casement fell and broke into tearing sobs.

"I can't . . . go . . . any farther. I can't! Oh, Clay . . . I'm sorry . . . sorry. . . ."

He lifted her up, pulled her into the circle of his arm. "Steady, Kitts. We're still doing all right. Steady."

They went on down the ridge, slowly now, the girl sagging and stumbling. They struck a little saddle, which sloped up on the far side to an abrupt point. Here was a jumble of rocks, brush-fringed. Almost carrying the faltering girl, Clay worked a way into the heart of this cover before letting his companion slump down.

"We fort up here," he panted. "If the Goshiutes want to get us out of here, they'll pay a stiff price. But stay low, Kitts . . . where an arrow can't reach you. Don't be afraid. I'll be close by."

He left her there, silent, except for her labored breathing, while he prowled the limits of the point. On the upper side was that saddle, with its fairly even slope, but below and to the right and left the point dropped off abruptly. Any Goshiute working a way on to that point against a reasonably alert gun would earn his passage. Except for the dark. . . .

The upper side was the real danger point. A massed rush there, carried through determinedly could be bad. Clay found a spot where he could watch this approach and settled down.

The night was mocking, so still and empty and peaceful it seemed. But somewhere out there, beyond where a man's senses could reach, prowled something that turned a man's insides to water. There was a movement behind him, and then the girl's voice, low-pitched and taut.

"I've got to be near you. I can't stand . . . being alone."

"Sure," said Clay gently. "I understand. But keep low."

A man's eyes, under the strain of constant watching and looking and trying to pierce the mocking gloom, played him tricks. Several times Clay stiffened, half raised his rifle, as he thought he glimpsed a shift of movement out there, but each time it was nothing, after all.

And then, abruptly, there was movement, very real and not fancied. Vague shadows, moving through the thin starlight, coming down across the sweep of the saddle above the point. Clay settled the rifle against his shoulder, held low, blasted a shot, swung the lever of the Henry, shot again, and then a third time. The echoes rocketed across the night.

One of those advancing shadows doubled up and pitched forward. A second went down in a crazy, spinning fall, while a third, with a leg jerked from under, went floundering off to one side, half hopping, half crawling. The rest vanished like wind-blown wisps of fog, and a hair-raising mixture of sound lifted— muffled gobbles and grunts and a guttural chittering. A wild, shrilling war whoop would not have been nearly so unnerving as this pagan, animal chittering.

Now also sounded the short, thumping strum of bow strings, a whispering flutter, and then arrows were thudding against the rocks of the point and slapping through the thin brush. Clay pressed a hand against the girl's shoulder.

"Low," he warned. "Stay down."

For the better part of half a minute the arrows hissed and fluttered and thudded. Then across that open saddle of the ridge came racing figures, squat, elusive, malignant. Clay's rifle belted the echoes again. He missed one of the charging Goshiutes, then knocked the next two sprawling.

The rest broke and faded into the dark again. And now, as that nerve-jangling chittering sound lifted once more, it held a thin and baffled ferocity.

Abruptly all sound faded. Clay reloaded, blessing the genius of the man who had invented this repeating Henry rifle. This night, so far, it had made one man at least the equal of many.

Clay studied the night. What would the savages try now? Had their nerve run out, or were they up to some other kind of wild strategy? Were they gathering for another rush across that open saddle? Clay waited, some of the tautness running out of him. Abruptly he realized he was thirsty and he thought longingly of the water bag he'd had to leave behind, slung to the buckboard.

Kitts Casement was a silent presence beside him. With a cheerfulness he did not altogether feel, he murmured: "We're doing pretty well by ourselves. They've taken quite a chunk of punishment and they're not liking it too well. They could have decided they've had enough."

For a long time she did not answer, but when she did, she spoke an irrelevant thing. "I've so much to be sorry for. . . ."

The stillness grew oppressive as it hung on and on. Clay tried to figure the time by the swing of the stars. It was certain that midnight had passed and that this thin cold that was now settling in was the chill of early morning. If day and its welcome light would only hurry.

The Goshiutes had already found out the deadly meaning of an accurate rifle in the hands of a man who knew how to shoot it. They would hardly dare more against this combination in daylight than they had under the deceptive half light of the cold stars. It was a safe bet that, if they were going to do any more about this thing, they would make their try before dawn, or just at dawn. But how could a man know what they were up to now?

Clay slid his revolver from the holster, pressed it into the girl's hand. "I've got to scout a little, Kitts. Either they've pulled out or they're trying to make a sneak in from the sides or from below. In any case, I've got to find out, for I can't afford to let them get in too close. I won't be far away. If you see anything move, shoot . . . and I'll be right back with you."

He felt her free hand catch at him, as though to hold him back. Then the touch fell away and she murmured muffled words. "All right, Clay."

He moved off, working cautiously around the rim of the point, pausing at short intervals to pour straining senses across the night. He had almost completed a circle of the point when, from close below, he picked up the faintest slither of sound. He could see nothing, but when he listened, holding his breath, he picked up the sound again. And now there was odor touching his nostrils, a fetid, wild odor, combined of rancid grease and human sweat.

Clay felt around him and located a sizable chunk of loose rock. He judged distance carefully and tossed the fragment down. It struck with a thump and set up a slight crashing in a thicket of brush. And it brought a vague stir of startled movement not fifteen feet below. Clay dropped the muzzle of the Henry rifle into line and pulled the trigger. Behind the slashing echo there was a sighing grunt and something went rolling and tumbling heavily down the slope.

Close at Clay's right, on the very rim of the point, a figure lunged upright and sprang at him. Clay had no time to lever in another cartridge. He had only time to reverse his rifle, driving the steel-shod butt up and out, smashing it into the face of the charging savage. It struck with a wicked crunch, and the Goshiute sagged at Clay's feet.

But there was blind, cat-like tenacity of life in the Goshiute and clawing hands caught and jerked at Clay's legs. He had to use the pounding butt of the rifle twice more before this crazed, ferocious thing at his feet went still. And that sickening odor came up to him, clogging his throat.

Behind Clay there was a thrashing rush in the brush, and he whirled to glimpse the bulk of another plunging figure. He had just time to swing the lever of the Henry and pull the trigger, shooting from the hip, and this time his target was so close the lancing flame of the shot seemed to burn right into the squat bulk. So close it was impossible to miss.

And now Clay heard Katherine Casement cry in alarm and the revolver he'd left with her thudded heavily in three quick reports. He scrambled across the rocks toward her. "Kitts!" he yelled. "Kitts . . . !"

Just before he reached her, she shot again, up the ridge. Clay dropped in beside her, glimpsed movement out there, more clearly outlined than any before, and he flung a final shot. Then once more there was that repressed waiting which was silence, but also a queer sort of soundless thunder, which was the wild beating of a man's heart and the agony of his suspense. He put an arm about the girl's shoulders.

"You're all right?"

"All right. Right after . . . your first shot . . . back there, they started coming down the ridge again. I . . . I shot at them. There was one so close . . . I heard the bullet hit."

He felt her shoulders shake in sobbing relief. He pulled her close and held her so until she quieted. And the world looked strange in his eyes, for now all about him things were taking on distinctness and the space of distance began to open up and grow. Abruptly he understood. This was the dawn.

Time had run away. Time that always ran away and never stopped its speeding, no matter what any man's trivial conflicts and struggles and dangers might be. Time, which measured a man's years and passed him by and never came back. But it could also, on occasion, bring the greatest relief and comfort. Like now—when it brought the dawn.

Somewhere up above and thinned with distance, there lifted a sound as much animal as it was human. A single fading howl, thwarted, mournful as that of a wolf, disappointed in the hunt. And Clay understood the meaning of it. The Goshiutes had had enough. The survivors were leaving the field of battle. Dawn and the white man's guns were too much for them.

In the east, beyond the mountains, the sky began turning silver and old rose, flushing more strongly with every passing moment. Clay stood erect, lifting the girl with him.

"That's the end of them, Kitts. We can go on now."

This night had done things to her. It had thinned her face, put shadows in her eyes. Her cheeks were grimed, her coppery hair loose and awry, her clothes torn from headlong flight across rocks and through clutching brush. But as she stood there, facing the dawn with thankfulness, she was very fair in Clay Roswell's eyes.

Feeling his glance, sensing what was behind it, faint color warmed her wan face. "I'll never know terror again, Clay. I'm a lot older than I was. Yes, we can go now."

There were squat and wildly shaggy things lying silently on the ridge sweep above the point, and, as they passed them, Kitts averted her eyes and pressed close to Clay's side. But presently, swinging down and under the point, to pick up another ridge top that ran a winding way toward the gulf of desert below, they were clear of all sign of what had made such a grisly nightmare of the long hours passed.

The sun came fully up and flashed its quick warmth on them. And now, down below, winding into view from a defile's shadowed depth came a troop of United States cavalry. Clay fired a shot in the air and the lashing echoes brought discovery. The file of troopers came surging up toward them. Clay turned and smiled down into the girl's weary, haunted eyes.

"It's a new day, Kitts," he said.

CHAPTER EIGHTEEN

The cavalry troop threw a short camp, during which coffee and bacon were cooked and served. While he and Kitts ate, Clay told their story to a grizzled, hawk-faced officer, who ordered two of his men to turn their horses over to Clay and Kitts and then double up with two of their companions and ride escort for Clay and Kitts back to Fort Churchill. He and the rest of his troop would ride high and try and pick up the trail of the fleeing Goshiutes and, as he curtly put it, put more fear of God into them.

"They've already had a pretty stiff lesson, but perhaps we can add to it," he said.

At the moment of parting, the officer shook Clay's hand and gave Katherine Casement his best military bow. "You two have had a night to remember. A rough one, but a great one, as you'll realize when you recall it all, later on. And I've seen men decorated for less than what you've been through. My respects."

It was the same old desert, now that the sun was climbing high. Heat and dust and far distance. With let-down, the weariness of that long, wild night settled Clay deep in his saddle and he marveled anew at the endurance and courage of this slim, ruddy-haired girl riding beside him. He respected her silence, for he knew that her thoughts were reaching out ahead to her father, and, when the dusty bedlam that was Fort Churchill once more lifted out of the desert to meet them, he led the way directly to the Casement cabin, for it was a fair guess that this

167

was where Jack Casement would be.

He helped her down, steadied her a moment, for she was stiff and cramped and uncertain on her feet. She looked up and met his glance fully, with a strange and moving depth in her eyes. And she murmured just two words, but the way she spoke them drove the weariness from him and filled him with a swift and building warmth.

"Thank you."

Lafe Hubbard, the warehouseman, stepped from the cabin door. He stared in some amazement, then exclaimed: "You arrived at just the right time, Miss Kate! Your father is conscious and asking for you."

She hurried to the door, paused, and turned. "Clay, you're not to leave Churchill until I've had the chance to talk to you again. Promise."

Her words startled him, but he nodded. "I promise." She went on in. Clay turned the horses over to the troopers and thanked them. Then he faced Lafe Hubbard. "Jack Casement . . . he's making the grade?"

Hubbard nodded. "With any kind of luck he'll be out of the woods in another week. The best medicine in the world for him just went into the cabin. Sa-ay, by the looks of you, Miss Kate and you must have been through something."

"We have been, Lafe. It was quite a night. Now, what's the story about the shooting?"

Hubbard told him what he knew, which wasn't too much. He'd been at work in the warehouse, knowing that Jack Casement and Reed Owen were in the office, having an argument. He'd heard the shot, and, when he got to the office, Reed Owen was gone, while Jack Casement was down.

"Any idea where Owen disappeared to?" Clay asked. Hubbard shook his head. "Not a damn' one, except he sure lit a shuck out of town. When the word of the shooting got around, a bunch of teamsters went on the hunt for Owen. They combed the town from top to bottom and back up again, but they couldn't turn up hide or hair of him. There's no tellin' where he is now. Probably plumb across the Sierras somewhere, and still travelin'. For the boys swear that, if they lay a hand on him, they'll string him higher than they did Hoke Pickard. You aiming to do something about him, Clay?"

Clay's eyes pinched down. "Yeah, I do. But first I'm going to get some rest."

He went over to one of the bunkhouses, stretched out, and sought sleep. For a long time it wouldn't come. In the darkness behind his closed lids it seemed he could see again those drifting, shadowy figures of the past night, those squat and shaggy nightmare shapes, and in his ears still rang that outlandish chittering sound that suggested something almost inhuman. That he and Katherine Casement had won through unharmed was a wonder hard to clothe with reality. In time that unreality would grow until it would be easy to believe it was all something that had never taken place.

When sleep did take over, it was deep and long.

The singing of the bugles, carrying clearly down from the military post, woke him at day's end. By the time he had cleaned up and eaten, sundown had turned to twilight and twilight was thickening to deep dusk. He felt a strange and rewarding comfort as he went up to the Casement cabin and Katherine answered his knock. For she looked rested and all her crisp charm was back and she was good to look at.

"Just wanted to get the latest on your father, Kitts," he said. "And then you said you wanted to talk to me."

Her eyes were luminous with relief. "Dad's going to get well, Clay. He really is."

"That is going to be great news to carry back to the men on the job."

"Then, you're going right back, Clay?"

He shook his head. "No, Kitts. I've got another chore to do. Somebody else can take the word. I'm not really needed out there. Bill Yerkes has forgotten more about wagons than I'll ever know, and Tom Hughes is plenty big enough man to keep the rest of the job moving along."

She closed the door softly, came out, and stood beside him, there in the soft, warm dusk.

"I know what you have in mind. You're going after Reed Owen, aren't you?"

Clay nodded. "Somebody has to, Kitts. And. . . ."

"Why do they have to? What good would it do? Reed Owen just doesn't count any more. He doesn't count a bit. And wherever he is, his own punishment is riding with him. It will always ride with him. Dad's going to get well. Reed Owen has done his worst by us. He can't hurt us any more. It's better just to forget him."

Clay looked down at her, trying to figure what was behind her words. What hidden purpose of her own was this girl trying to serve? Could it be that, even after all that had taken place, she still owned to some lingering affection for Reed Owen? It was a conclusion that hardly made sense, yet who knew the vagaries of a woman's mind and heart?

Clay recalled that moment when, out by the headquarters wagon, she had faced him and thrown the lie at him and defended Reed Owen almost savagely, and the newly found comfort that had grown in him began to shrink and fade. His face turned bleak and his tone took on a shade of harshness.

"The man is already responsible for the murder of two good men, and the only reason he isn't the outright murderer of a third . . . your father . . . is because of the mathematics surrounding the course of a bullet and the fact that a good doctor was handy. Kitts, he can't be allowed to get off scotfree after that. Surely you don't want that?"

"I know exactly what I want, Clay Roswell . . . and it isn't at all what you think," she said steadily. "And I also know what I don't want. I don't want you to go after Reed Owen, Clay."

"But why, girl . . . why?"

"Because there are bigger things to be done, things which count much more. The main job, where you're needed much more than you think . . . where I know Dad wants you to be. Everything else is of small account beside that. Clay, Dad will be strong enough to talk to you in the morning. Will you be here?"

This girl. How the devil could a man refuse her a wish?

"All right," he said curtly, "I'll be here. But beyond that I'm not promising a thing."

He turned and stamped away. Kitts stood staring after him, a little smile on her lips, her eyes very soft.

Weariness came back to Clay as he moved away into the night. Again he asked himself—how could you figure a woman and the way her mind worked? Where a man would be thirsting for revenge against Reed Owen, Kitts Casement wanted this thing dropped and forgotten. Why should she feel that way about a treacherous renegade?

Maybe, he thought, it was because women hung on to old dreams and insisted on sugaring them up, no matter how bitter the taste. Maybe because when a woman had once known softness in her heart for a man she could never shut him entirely out of her memory, no matter how greatly he may have betrayed her trust and confidence. Hell! There were a million maybes and none of them supplied a satisfactory answer.

Chapter Nineteen

Another full night of sleep wiped the last shred of lingering weariness from Roswell. He was up early, and the dawn light was good in his eyes and the fading breath of night, crisp and sweet with space, filled his lungs with comfort. The old vigor was back, his eyes were clear, and the drawn lines of fatigue wiped fully from his face.

Breakfast tasted extra good and so did his pipe, and even the acrid bite of the dust kicked up by the shifting mules in the freight corrals seemed pleasant in his nostrils. Of a sudden it came to Clay what this country meant to him. He'd never thought much about it before, but now abruptly he stopped to consider it all.

The quest of a job riding Pony Express had started him West. Fate in the shape of the Pickard brothers had scotched that fine dream. Well, he'd more than evened with the Pickards for that. They were dead and gone and here he was, feeling as fit as ever in his life, and part of a job that, while not as spectacular and moving perhaps as the Pony Express, was one to serve the same purpose and serve it much faster and more handily. This job also would endure down the years, while the Pony Express was already living on borrowed time. The Pony Express would live in history, but the telegraph wire would live not only in history, but in its lasting self.

And the country itself, it demanded much of men, but it gave much in return to those who grew to understand it. This was a young land, bursting with vigor, and the lure of it grew on a man. It challenged him to show his best, and, if that best was good enough, it offered him open sesame. Clay stretched his arms and silently called down all the wild flavor of it. And found it good.

A couple of teamsters showed at a corner of the corrals and Clay called them over to him. One of these was the burly, grinning, blue-eyed young fellow who had led the group that had lynched Hoke Pickard, and now he eyed Clay with diffidence and a slight uneasiness. His companion asked: "What's the word of Jack Casement this mornin'?"

"Last night it was very good," Clay told him. "This morning it should be better. I understand some of you boys really combed the town looking for Reed Owen, but without any luck. And you've heard no word of him since?"

"If we had, he'd be dead by this time," said the blue-eyed one bluntly. "We had a rope along while we looked for him, and, mister, we looked. If there's a corner or possible hide-out in Fort Churchill we didn't pry into, I don't know where it is."

"This is mighty big country, and Owen's skipped these parts," said the other teamster. "I doubt any of us will ever see him again, more's the pity. That feller deserves stretchin' just as much as Hoke Pickard did. I still would like to know why he shot Jack Casement."

"That's something I can tell you now," said Clay. "I'll say this first. Owen deserves the rope more than Hoke Pickard did. Here's why." Then he went on to tell the whole story about Reed Owen. "I know that Jack Casement intended to call him to account," Clay ended. "And that's what probably led up to the shooting. I'll know for sure a little later, for I expect to talk to Casement this morning."

The blue-eyed teamster swore savagely. "Then Owen is just as much responsible for the deaths of Brad Lincoln and Danny

Huggins as the two Pickards were?"

"Just as much." Clay nodded. "Suppose you boys spread that word around. Here's my thought on that. One man might try and work out Reed Owen's trail, spend a lifetime at it, and still not come up with him. But a lot of men, looking and listening and dropping a word here and there . . . well, you never know when they might stumble onto a lead. You teamsters are a pretty clanny outfit, whether you're all working on the same job or not. Whether you're hauling for us or the Pony Express or even working the route clear across the Sierras, any one of you would feel pretty good if he turned up something that brought any man to an accounting who in any way had something to do with the murder of two of your trade. Get the idea?"

"Plenty," burst out the blue-eyed one. "Boss, that word will be spread, and, if any trace shows up anywhere, you'll hear about it. Now maybe this country won't be big enough for Reed Owen to hide out in, after all."

An hour after sunup, Clay went over to the Casement cabin again. Again Katherine answered his knock and again to Clay she seemed to shine in the sun.

"Thank you for coming as you promised, Clay," she said. "Dad's waiting to see you. The doctor has been and gone. He's quite happy about Dad, but said you mustn't talk too long. Five minutes is the limit."

Jack Casement was wan and white under the desert tan, but some of the old driving vigor showed in his eyes. He smiled grimly at Clay.

"Guess I should have let you come along with me the way you wanted to, boy . . . when I set out to face that fellow. He was a little too slick and fast for me . . . like he's been from the first. But he bungled the job. The sawbones says I'll be out again in time to watch some more of those poles march and more wire strung." Casement's voice was a little husky, but fairly strong.

"That we'll all be happy to see, sir," Clay told him. "But in the meantime, don't you go to worrying about progress. If I know those men out at point of wire . . . and I think I do . . . they'll be working twice as hard now, so's not to let you down."

Casement nodded. "I'm sure of that. Good men, all of them. Only one damn' rat in the whole outfit. Clay, I know what you have in your mind to do. Forget it. Reed Owen can wait . . . or go to hell in his own way and fashion. The job's the thing. I want you back out there. Oh, I know you think Bill Yerkes can handle the wagons as well as you. I don't. If I did, I'd have hired him as wagon boss instead of you. And you mean more than just wagon boss out there. You mean added help for Tom Hughes to keep things going. The real tough part of the job is still ahead and I need all my good men out there. When you leave this cabin, I want you to head straight for point of wire. You'll do it?"

Katherine stood across the sick bed from Clay. He looked at her, and she met his eyes steadily, faintly smiling. "You," he said, "are very clever, young lady." He looked down at Jack Casement again. "If that's the way you want it, sir, that's the way it will be. I'll head out right away."

"Thanks, lad," said Casement gruffly. "Thanks for so many things. Tell the boys I'll be along."

Casement sighed, like a man relieved of a worry. He closed his eyes. Katherine nodded her head, and Clay followed her softly out. There she faced him. "Again I know what you're thinking, and again you're wrong, Clay. I never put Dad up to that. It's just that he sees what is really important and what is not." Then she added softly: "I want to say what Dad just said. Thanks for so many things."

Clay caught a ride with a supply wagon that pulled out of

Fort Churchill within the next half hour. His mood brightened as the slow grind of the wheels put the miles behind. Work lay out ahead, and a man could lose himself in work. Work, he mused, was the greatest benefit conferred on mankind by an all-wise Creator. It gave point and purpose to existence. Without it a man would never know balance and the relief of life's urgings. For the things a man won from life by the measure of his own toil and at the price of his own sweat were the price of his own worth, not only in his own eyes, but in the eyes of all others who understood these things. Work built things, and in the building a man built himself.

Where the Goshiute attack had first struck, the buckboard had been taken away. But the dead horses lay by the side of the road and the coyotes and buzzards had been at work and the stench of carrion offended the air.

Then it was night again in the high silent hills, with a campfire gleaming ruddily and tired mules munching at the feed racks on the sides of the wagon. The comfort of blankets under the marching stars, and then another dawn's fresh breath and wheels rolling once more.

At the relay station at Cedar Springs Pass there was a message waiting for Clay, freshly arrived over the wire. It was brief but meaningful.

Don't let us down. We're with you in thought.

The Casements

Once more there was the long sage valley and the brooding ranks of other mountains beyond, where the marching poles and swooping wire were already beginning to storm those far slopes.

Bill Yerkes descended upon Clay with profane, gruff relief. "Boy," he growled, "you sure managed to scare hell out of all of us. When Pete Ryder, haulin' in from Churchill, found that buckboard and dead team full of Goshiute arrows and no sign at all of you and Miss Kate, and brought the word in, it was all Tom Hughes and I could do to keep every crew on the job from droppin' their tools and goin' on a grand Injun hunt. They were stormin' to run down every varmint within a hundred-mile radius of here. I told them not to go jumpin' the traces, that you'd cut your eyeteeth at that sort of thing, and that you'd probably turn up bright and sassy as usual. I was tellin' them things I wasn't none too sure of myself. But I was hopin' . . . and worryin' plenty. Must've been a tough time for you, particularly for Miss Kate?"

"It was a rough night, all right." Clay nodded. "And we were lucky. Kitts, well, she's Jack Casement's daughter. Which tells her part in the deal pretty well. She was great. Give you the whole story later."

He showed Bill the message he'd picked up at the relay station and the old teamster spread the word among the various crews, and they went at their tasks with renewed vigor. The old man, they said, would be with them again before the finish.

So they went up that far range of hostile mountains, crested them, and on down the other side. They built another relay station and moved out into another high sage desert. They ferreted out new timber stands where the pole-cutting crews labored. They hauled supplies and they strung wire and they took the worst the wilderness could offer and they beat it down and marched on over it. Time marched, too, days and weeks of it.

Fort Churchill, so distant now when measured by the roll of wagon wheels, was only seconds away by the magic of sun-glistened wire and clicking instruments and that strange invisible power that came out of ranks of fuming batteries. And so word of this and that came to them. They learned that the military was combing all the far country, that there had been several brushes with the Goshiutes and White Knives, that the fear of their pagan gods had been put into the savages by the hard-riding troopers. And so the long road miles became increasingly safe.

And then one day another message came over the wire. It was from Jack Casement to Clay Roswell. It said:

Bring the headquarters wagon back to Churchill. I'm ready to go.

Clay showed the message to Bill Yerkes. "Pick a good sound man for the chore, Bill."

"Now mebbe you better read that again," drawled Bill. "It doesn't say send, it says bring. And the message is to you, boy. I figger it means what it says. Your chore, Clay."

So Clay left the next morning, driving the big spring wagon behind a team of four. And he thought, as he drove, that a man had to make this drive to get full realization of how far the job had progressed. Churchill was mightily distant to a man who had to drive a wagon there.

So now it was September and the day was dusty and wickedly hot and there was Fort Churchill once more, lifting out of the shimmering, relentless sun beating down. Clay rolled the headquarters wagon up to the freight corrals at the edge of town and turned the team over to the care of a hostler, slapped the dust from himself, and went over to the Casement cabin. At his knock it was Jack Casement's voice that hailed him in.

Casement was thinner than Clay had ever seen him, but his eyes were clear and his step steady as he came across the room to shake Clay's hand.

"Lad," he exclaimed, "you sure look good to me! I call it one of the high-luck days of my life when you walked into it. Lord! You're a brown, lean, hungry-looking specimen."

Clay grinned. "This country can sure whip a man down to

whang leather. You're looking fine yourself, sir."

"Not yet quite my old self," said Casement wryly. "But I will be. Fuming and stewing to get back on the job are no substitutes for the sun and a campfire and a camp lying still and resting under the stars. Give me a couple of weeks of that and I'll be right back up to snuff. How's the job going?"

Clay had brought a surveyor's map with him and now he spread this out on the table and pointed to a pencil check on it. "Right there was the exact point of wire when I left. Tom Hughes and I kept the records and reports up as best we could, but I warn you, you and Katherine have a chore of paperwork ahead of you."

"Don't care if there's a mountain of it," declared Casement, "just so I can get out there again." He studied the map keenly, made a few swift computations of time and distance. "Hell, lad, we're out a good three or four miles ahead of scheduled progress. Maybe I better stay right here and let you and Tom keep on running things."

"No credit due Hughes and me, sir," vowed Clay. "That's a present of the men to you. Ever since you got laid up, all the gangs have been giving a few extra licks. They'll sure be glad to see you back on the job."

"We leave early tomorrow," said Casement. "And I just can't wait. Kitts is over at the warehouse office, getting things in shape. Don't know what I'd ever do without that girl of mine. Which reminds me of something else."

Casement went silent for a moment, sobering. "Last time I saw you, Clay, I didn't know anything about what you and Kitts went through when those cussed Goshiutes jumped you. I wasn't quite in shape then to hear that news. But Kitts told me all about it, later. What the hell can I say to you about that, lad? You brought my girl safely. . . ." He paused, shook his head. "I still get the cold shivers every time I think of what the end of that affair could have been. One way or another you've the knack of putting the Casement family mighty deep in your debt."

"Any one of the men would have done as well as I did, probably better," said Clay gruffly. "Kitts was great. Plenty of women would have gone plumb to pieces, been helpless and useless. But not Kitts. Er . . . any word come through at all about Reed Owen?"

Casement shook his head, taking a turn up and down the room. The old blaze shone in his eyes and his face pulled grim. "No, he's dropped completely from sight. But I haven't forgotten him and I never will. I'm not a revengeful man and I can forgive a lot of things. But never what Reed Owen added up to. The job comes first with me, as it has from the first. That must be finished and it will be finished. After that . . . well. . . ." He opened a hand fully, then clenched it tight.

His mood changed to bright eagerness again. "Let's go up to the warehouse and see Kitts. She'll be wanting to get some gear ready for the trip out to the job tomorrow. This time, I doubt she and I'll see Churchill again until the job is done."

Clay watched this man walking beside him, watched the way he tipped his face to the sun, the way he breathed deeply of the hot but healing air. And Clay thought that here was a man who would never be confined long by four walls. Here was a man big in his thoughts and dreams and ambitions, a man to do big things in a big way in a big country. When this job was done, there would be others like it that needed doing. And at the forefront of those jobs, Jack Casement would always be somewhere about. Clay wondered how closely his own destiny in the future would be linked to that of Jack Casement.

Kitts met them at the office door. She was completely her old self, poised and capable and sure. Clay's heart leaped when he saw her and he didn't realize until now how eager he'd been for sight of her again.

"Dad," she said, excitement in her voice, "we'll be leaving for point of wire soon. I can tell that by the look of you."

"Bright and early tomorrow morning, Kitts." Casement nodded. "So you better knock off here and get your gear ready. We won't be back until the job's finished."

She faced Clay and impulsively gave him both her hands. "Clay," she said simply, "it's so good to see you."

She held his glance for a moment, then faint color beat through her cheeks and she pulled away behind a curtain of reserve. "Dad's been driving me crazy, Clay, grumping around because he didn't get well faster. If there's anything crankier than a sick man getting well, I don't know what it is."

"Hah!" exclaimed her father. "You should throw rocks at me, young lady. You've fretted just as much as I have. Think I haven't noticed the way you'd stand and stare for minutes out to the east? You've been just an anxious as I have to get back to point of wire."

She laughed softly. "I stand convicted. Clay, how are all my old friends . . . like Bill Yerkes, for instance?"

Clay grinned. "Ornery as usual. Bill's always giving me hell about something. I've thought of firing him, half a dozen times."

"You wouldn't dare. He's one of my prime favorites."

Clay's grin became a chuckle. "Fond of the old maverick, myself. He's pretty handy to have around."

Kitts turned to her father again. "There's nothing further to do here that really amounts to anything, Dad. So I'm taking your advice about getting my gear ready for tomorrow morning. I hope you'll appreciate someday how difficult it is for a woman to live for weeks on end out of a spring wagon without becoming something to frighten little children. Clay, I'll expect you at supper."

She hurried away, her coppery head shining in the sun. Clay and Casement went into the office and took over. They spent

181

the better part of the afternoon there, talking over what lay ahead. The final drive was coming up. Word had come through by Pony Express, so Casement said, that the west-running leg of the telegraph line, coming out of Salt Lake, was already far out in the salt flats.

"The original plan and estimate," he explained, "called for a tie-in just south of the Pony Express station at Deep Creek, east of Antelope Valley. The way things are going, that looks to be just about right, give or take a few miles. An all-over time of about four months for the actual job. Five hundred and seventy miles for the whole stretch, when the tie-in is effected. Future history will make quite a note of that, lad."

"That's what Alex Majors of the Pony Express told me when he advised me to try for a job with you," Clay agreed. Then he grinned. "Funny thing, but I don't feel that I'm helping in any way to make history. All I feel is just a sense of satisfaction every time I see another pole planted and another sweep of wire shining in the sun."

"Man," philosophized Jack Casement, "is a queer sort of brute. By and large he's a long way from being perfect and there are certain specimens among him that are of a pretty low order. Yet at times he shows a streak of pure nobility. Tell that to some horny-handed, sweating bully boy with a crowbar in his hands, fighting hard rock and cussing every inch of it while he digs another hole to set up another pole, and he'd swear you were crazy. But it's there, just the same. When man wants to really set his shoulder to a tough job, he generally rates up in the end as quite a guy."

"I'll feel a lot nobler after I've found a barber and got out of some of this shagginess." Clay grinned. "If I showed up at her supper table like this, I wouldn't blame Kitts a bit if she took a shot at me. Me for town."

He found the barber and was shaven and shorn and emerged

on the street where the long shadows were running and the dusty air seemed to quiver with the high, thin singing of the bugles from the military post. He recalled things he needed for himself and several items he was to pick up for several of the men out at wire's end. So he sought a trading post and by the time he had collected all these and carried them out to the headquarters wagon, the sun was fully down and it was time to report to the Casement cabin again.

Kitts Casement was her usual capable self in the kitchen, and, when they sat down to the savory meal, Clay thought back to the first time he'd sat at this same table, and he mused at all the water that had flowed under the bridge since that time. Life, it seemed, could certainly throw an unpredictable pattern at a man.

That night, right over there, Reed Owen had sat. But if Kitts Casement had any feeling that a ghost was at the table with them, she showed no sign of it. She was full of bright energy and cheerfulness, eager as a child over the prospects of tomorrow. Yet, despite this open manner, Clay couldn't get away from the feeling that there was an indefinable, but definite wall of reserve about her.

Later that night, while smoking a final pipe under the stars before turning in, he pondered this and again tried to find a reason. And ended up as confused and irritated as ever.

Knowing that Jack Casement meant every word of it when he said he wanted an early start, Clay brought the headquarters wagon to a stop at the cabin door while the late stars were still in the sky and only the faintest streak of gray was beginning to show along the eastern horizon. Even so, Jack and Kitts Casement were ready. There was considerable luggage to be stowed, but, as soon as this was done, they were off, the three of them on the wide seat.

A mile from town and the desert took them over, the lingering freshness of the past night cool against their faces. To their left marched the poles and the measured sweeps of the wire and in the slowly growing light the desert lay, vast and still and peaceful.

"This is good . . . good," observed Jack Casement heartily. "There were times when I cussed the desert with its heat and its dust, but I never will again. A man has to lay in a damned sickbed for weeks on end to appreciate something like this."

Driving the outfit, Clay did not forget that, although Jack Casement was completely out of the shadows, he still lacked much of his old-time strength and vigor and that the softness of convalescence still lay in his muscles. So Clay drove carefully, dodging the rougher stretches of the road where he could.

With the arrival of the midday hours, Casement's enthusiasm and ebullience of spirit faded somewhat and his face pulled into tired lines. Clay missed none of this, and he made early camp on a flat not far from the little sand valleys. He swung the wagon to throw a maximum of shade and spread a thick pad of blankets for Jack Casement to rest on. He shrugged off Casement's objections to this early stop.

"Plenty of time, Mister Casement. Tomorrow is another day."

"Feel like a damn' infant," grumbled Casement. "Have to be petted and pampered." Just the same, he sighed with deep content as he stretched out on the blankets.

Clay went quietly about setting up camp for the night, breaking out the water barrel, unharnessing and feeding the team. Sitting cross-legged beside her father, Katherine Casement watched Clay guardedly as he went about the frugal camp chores, seeing a tall man of soft and easy movement, Indian dark from wind and sun, his expression somber and taciturn. Virtually no word at all had passed between Clay and herself throughout the day; he seemed to have locked himself away in some corner of his mind that no one else could enter.

By the time sundown came and Clay built up a small fire, Jack Casement was sound asleep. As she began to prepare supper, Katherine said softly: "We won't disturb him. He'll be ravenous, come morning, but sleep is the best thing for him right now."

They ate in the early dark, the two of them, the fire's light a cheery, ruddy cone. After, while Katherine took care of the dishes, Clay made the rounds of camp again, making sure that all was secure for the night. He watered the team, rubbed them down. By the time he had finished this, the fire had died to gray ash and the girl had gone into the wagon for the night. Clay spread his own blankets a little apart, close to the throbbing, breathing earth. There were those who claimed that a man gathered strength, sleeping close to the earth. He wondered if they were right.

During the next day they passed a spot where the two horses had died, full of Goshiute arrows. Nothing was left now but some scattered bones and a few shreds of hide, dried iron-hard by the sun. Clay said nothing, but wondered if Kitts Casement would notice and remember? A swift glance at her face told him that she had and did. For she had paled a little and the breath beat faster in her throat and there was a wide and solemn shadow in her eyes.

Jack Casement stood the rigors of that day's drive better than he had the first, and the third day better than the second. So they came to Cedar Springs Pass where Casement got a whooping welcome that brought a broad grin to his face.

And so they went on and on, along the great sage valleys and over the mountains beyond and down to that next high desert, and finally they were once more up at point of wire. That night the crews threw an impromptu celebration over Casement's return to the job, and Casement shook many calloused palms

185

and traded banter with grinning, shaggy men. Kitts stood beside her father, smiling and smiling and once or twice furtively wiping her eyes.

Clay moved quietly in the background, where Bill Yerkes presently joined him.

"We were movin' pretty fast before, boy," said Bill. "But watch the fur fly now. Feller from the Salt Lake gang rode in yesterday, full of brag about how they're aimin' to hit Deep Crick before we do. He made a lot of bets with the boys on that. And now, with those bets hanging and with Jack Casement back, you're going to really see action."

Action it was. The end was in sight and a challenge had been made. The crews were at it in the first light of dawn and they stayed at it until night's dark closed them out. Everybody gave everybody else a helping hand. This thing was a race now, and the fever of it took hold of all.

Clay was no exception. He helped dig holes, helped lift poles into position. He dragged at long lengths of shining wire, passed tools up to the wire stringers, who went up and down poles with reckless speed. Men griped or railed not at the driving toil, but only when some momentary tie-up occurred, when all hands pitched in to straighten matters out and get things going again.

A teamster who was a little tardy in bringing up a load of poles got an all-over blistering from a dozen sources that left him bug-eyed and scorched and half in fear of his life. Clay grinned when he noted that with the next load that teamster was not only on time, but was able to wait a little before a crew could get the load off his wagon. Then it became the teamster's turn to scorch a few hides, which he did with a relish. In return he got no anger, just rough laughter and banter. The spirit was tremendous.

And so they surged on and on and they moved out of the high desert and into more lonely, barren hills and across these and down toward Deep Creek and the tie-in. Time had marched, too. September was gone. This was October and the hastening season tempered the heat by day and deepened the nights with chill. One day a gray haze wiped the usual brassiness from the sky. The next, rain fell for twelve hours and the next night was one of dank discomfort. But the sun was on the job again the next morning and the world steamed and the sage shone, clean-washed and filled the air with its pungency. Behind them, the mountain crests showed a cap of white. After that, men crawled out of blankets stiffened with frost and the glow of campfires took on added meaning and comfort.

These final weeks brought Jack Casement all the way back. Once more he was brown and tough and a driving spark always at the lead of things. There were days on end when Clay Roswell did not get a glimpse of him, or of Katherine Casement, either. But now and then he was able to move up to their evening fire for a little time.

Jack Casement was all business, completely absorbed in the job and its nearing finish. As for Katherine, it seemed to Clay that she had acquired a certain shyness. She was always soft-voiced, pleasant, but there was always that wall of reserve there. And after a visit with them, Clay would go away carrying within him a strange and gnawing emptiness that left him somber and silent.

A day came when one of the wire-stringing crew, working at the top of a pole, broke off in his work to stare out to the east. Then he pointed and shouted and the word spread that the Salt Lake working party was in sight, coming down the far slope toward Deep Creek. After that, men no longer walked as they worked. They ran.

Two days later it was done. The gangs met, shook hands, argued over who had reached Deep Creek first. That part didn't really matter, and everybody knew it. The big job was done.

Over the space of a few short months a generous slice of a continent had been tied together by an unbroken filament of metal, a strand of wire that sang under the push of the lonely wilderness winds. It seemed so fragile, that wire, yet it held a medium of strength beyond all measurement.

When the word was flashed, there would be celebrations in some places, but out here at the tie-in, after their first burst of enthusiasm, men grew quiet before the knowledge that the thing was done. The thing that had absorbed their every waking moment for months on end was finished and for a time their lives seemed hung in a vacuum.

Clay Roswell, considering the full significance of this moment, remembered something that Alex Majors had told him that first day in Fort Churchill. Now it had happened. When those two converging wire ends were spliced together, the Pony Express died, moved on into history. No more those lean and reckless riders flying through the day and through the night, no more the racing hoofs, beating out the lonely miles. No more the romance and the color and the dash. Time marched, the world turned, men lived and died, and history was written.

There was nothing to be done now but return to where they had started. So they gathered up their tools and their gear and stowed these in the wagons, climbed in themselves, and started the long trek back. For a time they found some interest in talking over various aspects of the job; certain points that they passed reminded them of an incident of some kind, and they discussed this. But gradually they grew silent and only occasionally lifted their eyes to the visible proof of their accomplishment. Wire across the desert, across the mountains. Singing wires.

CHAPTER TWENTY

The buckskin was tough and hardy and its steadily jogging hoofs carried Clay Roswell far out ahead of the slower, plodding wagons. And in the shortening hours of another fast-running afternoon, Clay heard the military bugles sounding retreat as he pulled in at the corrals at Fort Churchill. He left his horse there and went straight to the office of Alex Majors and found that tired, bearded man there alone.

"So the Pony Express is dead, sir," said Clay. "And I helped kill it. And I'm sorry."

Alex Majors smiled. "Don't be, son. We've had our day, served our purpose. We're satisfied. Like I told you before, the world moves. And men and their affairs must move with it. What's ahead of you now?"

"Don't know, sir," answered Clay soberly. "Hadn't thought about it too much. A job draws you in, takes all your time and thought, and, then, suddenly is done. And for a time after that a man sort of dangles, a little uncertain."

Alex Majors nodded. "Know exactly what you mean. I'm more or less in that spot myself right now. But you stick with Jack Casement. He was a big man before and he's still bigger now. Others know of this. There'll be lots of jobs ahead for Jack Casement. You ride with him and you can't go wrong. In the meantime, don't think about anything. A rest will do you good. About a job being done, well, there's a satisfaction but there is also a queer, strange sadness. But a little time always cures that.

And soon a new trail beckons and a brand-new enthusiasm for a brand-new project takes over and then a man finds himself going ahead once more. That's the way it will be with you, son."

Taking a turn through town in the gathering dusk, Clay mused over Alex Majors's words. The man spoke from experience, no doubt. But there were angles of the future that Alex Majors didn't know about. He didn't know about Katherine Casement and the spot she had come to occupy in Clay's consciousness. How she could stand within a stride of him and yet be so far away, because of that wall of reserve that she had lifted between them.

There was punishment here for a man, that would always be here while she was around. And she would be wherever Jack Casement was. And so, if he stayed on with Casement, then there would always be that punishment. Maybe the best thing for him to do was cut and ride. Over the Sierras, probably, and see what kind of country lay beyond them.

Fort Churchill seemed a little quieter than was its usual wont. It was still dusty and careless and brawling, but somehow it seemed a little subdued. Perhaps this was because it somehow sensed what history had in store for it, now that the Pony Express was dead, and that the business of a nation would no longer flow through it, but pass by overhead through swooping wire. Maybe it knew that history had written that it should die, as the Pony Express had, and that only its ghost would remain.

Sunk in his brooding thoughts, Clay strode past a shadow-blackened gap between two buildings, and it was then that a voice struck harshly out at him.

"I've been waiting for this, Roswell."

There were many things in that voice besides the ominous words spoken. There was hate, a raw thirst for vengeance, and frustration's corrosive acid. There was brooding, raw deadliness and the hoarseness of whiskey. But it was still the voice of Reed Owen.

A rotund, red-faced citizen of the town, carrying a stiff cargo of whiskey, came weaving by, and never knew the break this fact gave Clay Roswell, nor dreamed of the stark drama building up at his uncertain heels. But his position at that exact moment gave Clay a chance to come fully around and face the angle of threat under the cover of the drunk's wobbly course. And when the drunk had gone on, Clay was set and tautly alert for whatever danger was reaching for him from the shadows.

He had the tall bulk of Reed Owen focused solidly with every sense. He could make nothing of the man's face in that uncertain, fading light, but that didn't matter. The rest was clear enough.

Strange currents ran through Clay, his mind going blank in some ways and needle-sharp in others. It was as though the mechanics of a man's brain, in the face of stark danger, automatically shed all diverting thought and poured everything into that fine and probing concentration he now felt. He spoke, hardly realizing it.

"Come out in the open, Owen. For once in your life come out where a man can have a full look at you."

"Good enough for me . . . here." And as Reed Owen spoke, his hand made a stabbing forward movement, pale flame licked out, and a gun's report flung flat echoes across the street.

There was no immediate pain, only a smashing blow. It landed to one side, halfway down Clay's body, and it spun him back, reeling. For the moment it seemed to Clay that his muscles were locked, that only an ingrained sense of balance kept him on his feet at all, while no other part of his body would work. Then this paralysis broke as suddenly as it had struck, and somehow the Dragoon Colt that he'd carried so long was in his hand.

191

He came spinning back to face fully that menacing figure in the shadows and the big gun in his fist was rocking and bucking in recoil and its hoarse echoes were rolling. The voice of that gun swallowed everything. Not even the wild, terror-stricken yell of the startled drunk got far against those dominant, deadly echoes.

And now, finally, Reed Owen did come out into the open, a shaggy, shambling whiskey-bloated figure, ragged and filthy as a Siwash. It seemed to Clay's dazed eyes that the man was walking straight into the lashing flame of the Dragoon Colt.

Only there was no steadiness, no sureness to Reed Owen's stride. His steps were dragging, stumbling, with his knees bending more and more with each step he took.

The Dragoon Colt bellowed a final time. Reed Owen stopped in mid-stride and seemed to hang there, lifted on his toes. And then those bending knees gave way completely and let him down on his face.

Gun silent and sagging in his hand, Clay Roswell stood motionlessly for a long moment. A million years of time seemed to have been thrown at him in these few, brief thunderous seconds. And he was tired. God, how tired he was.

What was the matter with him? Where had his strength gone? He couldn't have lifted that Dragoon Colt level again to save his life. In fact, it had grown so heavy he couldn't even hold onto it—he had to let it drop.

And now things were whirling about him, wilder and wilder. The drunk was yelling, off key and crazy. Everything was crazy. The town's first lights, buildings—everything. The street was looping up and down like a writhing snake.

Another blow hit him, a blow cushioned with dust. Why, this was the street itself he was lying on. The earth. He was down. How did he get here?

Now the numbness in his side was lifting and in its place

came pain, raw waves of it sweeping through him. There was faraway shouting and it was growing dark . . . dark. . . .

He knew pain again. Some damned devil with red hair and bristling red whiskers was jabbing a spear into him and leering at him in his writhing torture and he cursed that devil in weak rage. Until the pain blotted everything out again.

This time the darkness lifted slowly; he had the feeling of floating up out of a pit of it. There was still pain, but not like it had been. And he had never known the earth to be so soft. Or was this the earth he was lying on? This posed a tremendous question that he tried to figure out as he lay in this strange half world where things were real, yet unreal.

He got his eyes open at last and looked up at a tremendous bulk of a man, a man with red hair and red whiskers who grinned down at him amiably.

"You," blurted Clay weakly, "should be a devil by rights. A devil with a spear jabbing at me. . . ."

The red-headed man chuckled. "Never took a finer cussing out in my life. Had to go deep to get that slug, but I got it. Now shut up and sleep and don't think about anything, or I'll really manhandle you."

This was easier to do than Clay thought it would be, just to lie still and sleep. He'd never felt so beat out and bushed before in his life. Sleep was awfully good.

When he awoke, everything was strongly real again. Everything was certain. He discovered he was lying in a bed with white sheets in a little room subdued and comfortable with its stillness and half light. There was a faint stir by the bed and he rolled his head and saw Jack Casement and Bill Yerkes, standing there.

Bill Yerkes said huskily: "Damned wild young bucko. Always scaring hell out of a man. Boy, how are you?"

"Good enough," murmured Clay. "Where am I?"

"Now where do you think?" growled Jack Casement. "Safe in the Casement cabin. You ended the trail, didn't you?"

"He was laying for me," Clay said. "Looked like he'd been living in a treetop with a whiskey bottle. He got the slug into me before I could do a thing about it. After that, things were pretty fast moving and jumbled. I don't remember all of it."

"Don't try, lad," said Casement. "Just forget all of it, take things easy, and get well."

Katherine Casement came into the room. "Clear out, you two," she told her father and Bill Yerkes. "You know what that military doctor said."

"Yeah, I know, Kitts." Casement grinned. "He said he'd done a first-class job of fixing on a very profane character. You sure learned a vocabulary from the muleskinners, Clay . . . according to the doctor."

"Clear out, I said," ordered the girl. "You can talk all that nonsense over later."

So Jack Casement and Bill Yerkes went out, and then there was only this quiet room, and Kitts.

She put an arm under his head, lifted him up, and gave him a drink of cool, sweet water. Then she fluffed his pillow and let him gently down on it again. After which she sat on the edge of the bed and looked at him.

Despite that sore and bandage-stiffened side, Clay squirmed under that direct regard. "I let you down, Kitts," he said lamely. "But I didn't go hunting for him, honest I didn't. He was laying for me and he came at me all of a sudden, and well. . . ."

She laid cool fingertips on his lips. "You let nobody down, Clay. What else could you do but what you did? Surely you don't think I'd ever hold a thing like that against you?" She hesitated, almost shyly, then went on. "In some things you've been a very obtuse individual, Clay Roswell. When I asked you not to try and hunt down Reed Owen, it was because . . . because I was afraid that . . . that he might succeed where the Goshiutes failed. And . . . he nearly did."

She blinked, brushed a hand across her eyes. Clay reached up and captured that hand. "So you remember that night, Kitts?"

"Remember it? How could I ever forget it. The mountains, the dark . . . the Goshiutes creeping in. A terrible night, but also a wonderful one. I learned so much about myself, that night. . . ."

"So did I, Kitts," said Clay. "I learned that no two people could go through such an experience together without forever after being tied together by some deep and lasting bond. But with me it began long before that. I can see now that it started with me that very first day, when I picked you up bodily and chucked you out of the way of that loose log. Remember?"

It might have been the tears that made her eyes glisten so. But also they were very soft. So were her lips when they came down to meet his. And her coppery hair was a sun-sweetened glory falling across his gaunt cheeks. . . .

ABOUT THE AUTHOR

L. P. Holmes was the author of a number of outstanding Western novels. Born in a snowed-in log cabin in the heart of the Rockies near Breckenridge, Colorado, Holmes moved with his family when very young to northern California and it was there that his father and older brothers built the ranch house where Holmes grew up and where, in later life, he would live again. He published his first story—"The Passing of the Ghost"—in *Action Stories* (9/25). He was paid 1/2¢ a word and received a check for $40. "Yeah . . . forty bucks," he said later. "Don't laugh. In those far-off days . . . a pair of young parents with a three-year-old son could buy a lot of groceries on forty bucks." He went on to contribute nearly six hundred stories of varying lengths to the magazine market as well as to write over fifty Western novels under his own name and the byline Matt Stuart. For many years of his life, Holmes would write in the mornings and spend his afternoons calling on a group of friends in town, among them the blind Western author, Charles H. Snow, who Lew Holmes always called Judge Snow (because he was Napa's Justice of the Peace in 1920–1924) and who frequently makes an appearance in later novels as a local justice in Holmes's imaginary Western communities. Holmes produced such notable novels as *Desert Rails* (1949), *Summer Range* (1951), and *Somewhere They Die* (1955) for which he received the Spur Award from the Western Writers of America. *Roaring Acres* (Five Star, 2007) marked his most recent appearance. In these novels one finds the themes so basic to his Western fiction: the loyalty that unites one man to another, the pride one must take in his work and a job well done, the innate generosity of most of the people who live in Holmes's ambient Western communities, and the vital relationship between a man and a woman in making a better life. His next Five Star Western will be *Orphans of Gunswift Graze.*